BEFORE THE END

STORIES FROM THE WORLD OF CEDAIN

JOHN PALLADINO

Before the End: Stories from the World of Cedain

© 2024 John Palladino

Editing: Sarah Chorn, www.sarahchornedits.com
Proofreading: Jim Scriven, YouTuber (Channel: Fantasy for the Ages)
Interior Formatting: Amber Helt, www.rootedinwriting.com
Cover Artist: Dusan Markovic, www.markovicdusan.com
Cover Design: Jake Caleb, www.jcalebdesign.com
Map Design: @sa_designs_inc

ISBN hardcover: 979-8-9862737-8-5
ISBN paperback: 979-8-9862737-7-8
ISBN ebook: 979-8-9862737-6-1

www.johnpalladino.com

CONTENTS

This is for Jim Scriven —a very special thank you for helping me in a pinch.

And, of course, for all the fans who've continued onwards from the first book. Thank you for the amazing support.

CYROK
THE FROSTED SPIRES
VOX
COLDRIDGE
TIMBERGLADE
THE S
ALEKI
GYRLOFT
BRYN
ANEPOLIS
PINECREST
ZEMUR
CALRYM
LOCHWALL
LARGOS
VALKRYND MTS
KELM
ILIDROS
VESSIA
ARGOA
HATHORAN
VALAKUR

R SEA
ARGATE
QELT
WARWIN
QOTHE
MACEPORT
YORDIV
ANDORA
BARIO
REMERIA
ASHMOUNT
THE ASHWOOD
AUCHESTER
SULTIVA
RIVANE
N
W
E
S
CEDAIN

A ROYAL MISSION

It burned, as it always did. And for once, Captain Decklin Hoarst let out a barking cough.

"Heh, for once it got *you*," Tekth said. He was one of those people with a wide face and a wider smile.

Decklin slammed the shot glass back on the table, picked up another, and tipped it back. Straight down the gullet. His mouth roared in fury. Warmth descended through his body. He smacked his lips and licked his whiskers. No sense in wasting it. Wiped his mouth with his jacket.

They were in a tavern of some sort in Coldridge. Decklin didn't know its name. He came here every night and still didn't know what to call it.

Decklin's head lowered, his chin bouncing off his collarbone. He snorted once, spat on the floorboards to his left, missed, and hit the wall instead. Snotty mucus clung to wood.

"Another one, Deck?" Tekth asked.

Always with the asking. It's why Decklin preferred to drink alone. He nodded and tried to grab the third shot glass sitting in front of him and missed. Took another swipe at it, missed again. "Fuck." He shook his head. "How many drinks are we at?"

"Twelve?"

After his third attempt, his fingers closed around the glass and he grinned. "Cheers," Decklin said. He tried clinking the glass against Tekth's but missed. Tipped the drink back, straight down the gullet. His mouth roared in fury. Warmth descended through his body. He smacked his lips and licked his whiskers. No sense in wasting it.

Tekth followed suit. "You're a habitual fuck, you know?"

Decklin grunted, then shivered. Didn't matter how much whiskey one drank, the damned weather in Cyrok was always freezing. "Guess so."

Blinking, he looked around the tavern. Men laughed; women danced. Women laughed; men danced. Decklin rolled his eyes. Or perhaps he rolled his head. He had a particular disdain for other people, noisy ones in particular. *Particularly women who walk around like* that.

The barmaid walked past, bosom ready to burst from her clothing. She'd already declined him twice that night. She circled the tavern, made her way back in his direction.

"C'mere," he said, raising a finger. Maybe he raised two. He couldn't tell.

Two barmaids walked over. *No. One finger, one barmaid.* He'd figured it out.

"I don't think you need more, Captain," she said, hands on hips. As if she could make that decision for him.

"Three for me, three more for Sergeant Tekth," Decklin said.

"The both of you are already quite drunk."

"*Now.*" He used his proper voice. The one that implied, 'If you don't do as I say, I'll come back in the morning and trash the place.' Not that he'd done that in quite some time. But the threat loomed.

"Right," she said, and left.

Tekth shook his head. "You act more like royalty than a king, Deck."

Decklin grunted again.

"Act like a prick, and she bends over backward for you," Tekth said, shaking his head, surprised.

The room took a lap around Decklin's head. He closed his eyes, opened them again. Wiped his mouth with the alcohol-stained sleeve of his captain's jacket. His superiors would have many things to say about that. He couldn't care less.

"Gonna start calling you 'Royal.'"

"You're an idiot and you're drunk, Sergeant. An idiot drunkard."

"A drunken idiot?"

"Don't argue with me. I'm your superior." Decklin hiccupped.

"Yes, Captain Royal, cyr." Tekth saluted.

"Fuck you."

"Fuck you, cyr."

The barmaid returned, laid out three shots of whiskey in front of each of them. "These are your last."

"Fuck you," they said.

She left.

Decklin downed another shot. Straight down the gullet. The back of his mouth roared in fury. Warmth descended through his body. He smacked his lips and licked his whiskers. No sense in wasting it. Wiped his mouth with his jacket.

Tekth wobbled in his chair. "I don't know that I can finish my three."

"You drink the last three, then get out of here. That's an order, Sergeant."

"You're a prick, cyr."

"Sometimes."

Tekth downed his three shots, slapped the table with his palm, said, "Thanks, Royal," and stumbled out of the tavern.

Royal. There were worse names. Better than being called 'Deck.'

He looked down at the two remaining shots. Bile stirred within his body and decided he'd drunk enough.

Royal stumbled out of the tavern, glanced at the business's sign. The letters made circles, joined together. He couldn't make them out.

He shivered. "It's fucking freezing."

Boots crunching in the snow, he made it home after stopping to vomit once. Maybe twice. He couldn't remember. It didn't matter. Royal couldn't care less.

<hr>

Clearing the crusted muck from his eyes as early morning sunlight blinded him, Royal groaned. His nose wrinkled at the acrid odor of vomit and the stench of alcohol. He sat up in his bed and saw the remnants of last night's bile on the ever-stained captain's jacket he still wore. He put his boots on, strapped his sword to his belt, and left. Snow reflected the sunlight, creating an array of diamonds and rainbows, forcing him to squint. He grabbed a handful of the snow and wiped the puke off his jacket as best he could.

"No time for water, overslept," Royal muttered to himself. "Shit's Blessing has graced me, it seems. Gotta get down to the docks, report to the lieutenant."

He thought about the lieutenant and tried predicting what he might say. "'Fuckin' sake, Captain Hoarst, you smell like a donkey's ass,' Colms will say. Then I'll say yeah, long night, long night. 'You and Tekth need to get a hold of yourselves,' he'll say. Sure, sure, working on it. I'll try to be better. Tomorrow. 'You should try today,' he'll say. Yeah, but fuck it. 'Might lose your station,' he'll say." Royal laughed. They wouldn't remove his station. Weren't enough soldiers in the Cyroki military as it was.

He opened the door to the barracks, boot laces slapping against the wooden floorboards. He'd forgotten to tie them.

Great, just another thing to be reprimanded for. He could tie them, but somebody would see. It'd be over then. He walked across the room, ignoring several bellows of "Hey, Captain!" and "Good morning, Deck!" Royal stepped into the open door of his boss's office.

"Captain Hoarst, what the fuck is this?" Lieutenant Clayton Colms, hazy clouds floating about his face, gestured with the hand holding a rolled skachi leaf, an addictive substance that one could smoke or chew. Royal had no need for skachi—alcohol was far better. Colms sat at his oak table, leaning back in his chair. Several junior officers catered to the man's needs, the constant sound of chatter, boots clicking, orders being given, quills moving over parchment, and other annoyances. Royal disliked the barracks.

He looked down at his jacket, saw he hadn't gotten all the vomit out. Saw a lot of alcohol stains—didn't really need to see them, he could smell them easy enough. "Rough night, Clay."

"Rough night, *cyr*," the lieutenant said out the side of his mouth, rolled skachi between his teeth on the other side.

"Rough night, Clay."

"You know, you're a right pain in the ass."

"So I've been told."

"Got a bit of a fat one for ya today."

Royal sighed. He sat in the chair opposite Colms.

"Captain Hoarst, close the door."

He stood, closed the door, sat in the chair again.

Colms took another long inhale of skachi. Smoke started filling the room. Royal coughed. Colms glared at him. Royal straightened himself in the chair. The lieutenant was serious. *Not a good start.*

"Captain, we have a serious problem."

Royal scratched at his chafing lips. "Oh?"

"Sergeant Tekth."

"Aye, Tekth."

"He's made a very serious report. Filed it this morning."

Royal lifted a brow. Tekth didn't file reports. "Regarding?"

"*My* fuckin' leadership, Decklin." He puffed on the skachi again. "Claimed I'm incapable of leadership. Said a lot of slanderous things. Lies upon lies. You hear me? These things aren't to be taken likely. I'm being investigated by the higher ups."

"That's not good, cyr."

"No, no, it's fuckin' not, Decklin."

"Call me 'Royal.'"

"Royal? What the fuck are you on about?"

Royal shrugged. "That's what they're calling me now."

Colms shook his head. "I'm upset."

"I can tell, Clay."

"Cyr."

"Right. Colms."

"You better start showing me some respect, Captain. I have your balls in a vice and I could end your career right now. You have a decision to make in a minute and you best make the right one or you won't like the outcome." He pulled the rolled skachi out, examined it, took another puff, closed his eyes.

Royal blinked.

"Let's start over, Captain."

"Royal."

"Royal." He puffed again. The smoke had now created a blurry filter between the two of them. "I'm not losing my job."

"No, cyr."

"You don't want to lose yours, either."

Royal didn't respond. Why should he care if he lost his job?

"Without the job"—Colms pulled the skachi back out—"you won't have any income. Without an income, you can't afford the drink."

Well, that's true. He sat straighter, more rigid. "I'm not losing my job, either."

"Damn straight, Captain, damn straight. I need this problem taken care of. Whisked away."

"The report?"

"Tekth."

"So you want me to discharge him."

"I want you to get rid of him." Colms breathed out a large cloud. Watched it float over to Royal. *"Permanently."*

"That'd be murder, cyr."

"That'd be saving our jobs, Captain."

"Tekth didn't file the report, Lieutenant." Royal didn't know that for sure, but he did know Tekth. His friend wouldn't be that foolish to try to disrupt his comfortable job with money enough to drink every night. He suspected subterfuge, but didn't know who'd involve themselves in that. Didn't truly care, as long as he and Tekth kept their jobs.

"I don't care if he did or didn't—it's filed. The Falcon Knights will look into this. They'll pry. Get rid of the source, and nobody's going to care. If Sergeant Tekth remains living, they question him. He either explains the report or it's found he's not the one who filed it . . . do you have any idea what type of shitstorm that'll open? They'll discharge *all* of us if they go digging that deep." Colms leaned forward, elbows on his oak table, skachi withering away between his lips, dropping burned leaves over his lap.

Burning holes in his jacket. Nobody cares about his *jacket.*

"Discreet, Captain. It needs to be discreet. You have by the end of the week, when Cyr Oxhorn arrives. You know how serious she takes these things. With nobody to question, she'll have to leave it alone."

Royal grunted. "What's in the report, Clay?"

"Cyr," Colms corrected him.

"What's in it?"

"Damn it, Captain, proper address, *now!*"

"What's in it, *cyr*?"

"Fuck. It shouldn't be this difficult, Deck."

"Royal," he corrected Colms.

"Mother Avani, save me." Calling upon their goddess to save him was something Clayton Colms never did, as far as Royal knew. *Means he's shaken.* "The report, Royal, claims I've committed countless crimes." *You have.* "Fraud, embezzlement, forgery, bribery, smuggling, *fuckin' treason*, Royal." *All true.* "If Tekth doesn't disappear"—*conspiracy, murder*—"they'll have somebody hanged." *You.* Colms sniffed the skachi. "I'm not hanging, Royal. Not hanging. It'd be easiest for me to shift the blame onto my closest confidant." He meant Royal. *You fucker.* "Somebody that has access to my office, the loyalty of the men, somebody who drinks himself stupid every night—unreliable—somebody who could benefit greatly from my removal. And they'll believe me, Royal, bet your fuckin' ass they'll believe me." He puffed again. "You take Sergeant Tekth somewhere quiet, get rid of him, and you become just as safe as I do. I'll handle the investigation whenever somebody discovers his body. I'll just claim it's my man, my responsibility, and we take care of our own. Everyone'll eat that shit up. If not, Reinkath'll do a fine job in your stead." *You cold bastard.*

"I'll deal with it," Royal said. It was the only thing he could say.

"Good."

Royal nodded, stood.

"Oh, and Royal?" Colms said, moving the rolled skachi to the other side of his mouth. "Don't fuck me on this. I'll make sure you lose everything, ya hear? *Everything.* You won't have a single coin to your name. No alcohol. *Nothing.* I'll have Reinkath pay you frequent visits."

Asshole. The only other officer in the port town of Coldridge who drank more than Royal. *He'd probably get my position.*

"Oh, and I'd promote him just to piss you off."

Royal narrowed his eyes. The man couldn't read minds, Royal knew that. Colms wasn't a Magicus. The north didn't have mages. Too remote. Not enough need. A Healer or two, maybe.

"Is that understood, Captain?"

"Yes, Clay."

"It's *Cyr*, Royal, damn you."

"Colms." Royal saluted and exited the office, ignoring the angry shouts issued from his superior.

He spent the rest of the day thinking, while neglecting his normal duties. Colms could throw Royal to the wolves, no problem. The lieutenant had plenty of allies, and near everyone who spent their time around him would vouch for the man. He was their superior, and it'd be dangerous to speak out against him—not only could Colms bar them from any military position, but the lieutenant had influence with Coldridge's citizens.

That night when Royal entered the tavern, he took a table in the corner—a visible indication he didn't want anyone disturbing him.

A server approached, and Royal just held up three fingers. Moments later, the server returned, setting three shots of his preferred whiskey.

He took one and threw it back. Straight down the gullet. The back of his mouth roared in fury. Warmth descended through his body. He smacked his lips and licked his whiskers. No sense in wasting it. Wiped his mouth with his jacket. Regretted the move as dried vomit flecked off and he caught a whiff of the acidic bile.

He unclasped his sword belt and let it fall to the floor

before he kicked back the chair and leaned against the wall, hiding his face in the shadows. *Fuck Colms.*

The door to the tavern opened, shut. Several people distributed themselves at different tables. Royal noticed his potential replacement, Reinkath, sitting at the bar. Then he saw Tekth looking around and sitting at their normal spot in the tavern. *Fuck Colms.*

Royal glanced at his two remaining shots of whiskey. His mouth watered, but he stood, gathered his sword and belt, and left the tavern, avoiding Tekth's attention. He needed to focus on his mission regarding Tekth, rather than getting drunk. It'd be the first time in years he hadn't gotten drunk after his shift. *Fuck Colms.*

He went home, laid on his bed—captain's jacket and boots still on—and thought about what he needed to do.

Royal was certain Tekth hadn't filed the report. They'd spent far too much time in each other's company. Tekth wasn't ambitious, didn't care about who was a good leader or not. He just wanted to report, do his duties, and return to the bar. Same as Royal. Which meant somebody must've had a grudge against Colms or the Cyroki military based in Coldridge, or else they would've submitted the report under their own name. *But who?*

Could it be Reinkath? *Unlikely.* Reinkath was another favorite of Colms, doubtful the man would sacrifice his standing now. Plus the man was too much of a drinker to do anything so competent—Royal would know.

He ran through the other suspects in his head. Marchessa who'd complained about the lieutenant's smoking habits. *Doubtful.* Adavir who had a penchant for doing criminal things, often at the behest of the lieutenant. *That'd be a betrayal . . . Colms also favors Adavir. I wouldn't put it past the bastard, though.* Hurk received daily verbal abuse from Colms. *Possible.* Plenty of candidates. He wondered if one of them had a secret motive.

It didn't matter *who* wrote the report, Royal remembered. Colms specifically ordered him to get rid of Tekth, even if he didn't report the lieutenant.

There wasn't a person Royal cared more about than himself, or alcohol. He did have morals though. But to stand up for those morals? That was a different matter. If he stood up for them, he'd jeopardize himself. *Can't do that.*

He tried to sleep but found it to be restless. Images of Tekth's betrayed face as Royal killed him haunted in his dreams.

Royal woke.

This morning, unlike most others, he took the time to clean himself. He washed his jacket. Trimmed his beard. Filed his nails. Then he polished his boots, sword, belt buckle, and buttons on his uniform. Combed his hair, rinsed his mouth, and pinned his officer's medal on his jacket. He hated the thing. Made him feel as if he was gloating. Determined, he marched to the barracks, to the office of Lieutenant Clayton Colms.

The door to the office was closed. Captain Decklin Hoarst, in all his glory, stormed in, and slammed the door.

"Captain," Colms said, lighting a skachi leaf.

"Lieutenant."

Colms looked Royal up and down. "Captain Hoarst, what the fuck is this?" He gestured at Royal's captain's jacket. Cleaned, polished, shined medal winking at the lieutenant.

"Professionalism, cyr. May I sit?"

Colms waved an open palm at the chair across from him and leaned forward, elbows resting on the oak table between them. "Professionalism doesn't mean barging in here without knocking, Captain."

"My apologies, cyr," Royal said as he scooted the chair in,

clasping his hands together and setting them on the table in front of him. Polite-like.

"Is the deed done, Captain? That'd be miraculous speed, but a damned commendable job."

"No, cyr."

"That is why you're here." It wasn't a question.

"Correct."

"Proceed."

"Well, cyr—"

"I meant proceed with the mission. I see no reason for you to be wasting your time, Captain Hoarst."

"Royal."

"Captain Royal."

"Thank you, cyr."

"Shut up and do your job."

Royal clenched his jaw.

Colms sighed, inhaling a lungful of skachi and closing his eyes. He took a breath, another, then opened them again. "Now it's my turn to apologize, Captain. I understand the position I've placed you in. It's not a good one. Fuck, it's terrible. But it's what's necessary for the good of the town." *For the good of you.* "And it's in your best interest." *Only because you're forcing it to be.* "Complete the task, secure a significant raise, and don't mention it again. That's all you have to do."

"I can't kill Tekth."

"*Sergeant* Tekth."

"It's not right, Clay."

The lieutenant narrowed his eyes but let that one slide. "Plenty of things aren't right, Captain. I shouldn't have to worry about investigations." *But you should worry. You wouldn't worry if you weren't doing illegal things.*

"I shouldn't have to worry about my superior plotting to stab me in the back and discard me because of a filed complaint. A filed complaint, I might add, that likely tells the truth."

Colms snarled, slamming a fist on the table. The skachi leaf broken by his sudden bite, fell to the ground to smolder. "You listen here, Deck, I've had enough of this disobedience, this shit-starting fuckery. You have two choices. Your first— leave here, do your damned job, and complete your task. Your second—don't do it and face the consequences, which will result in a lost job, no income, no booze, and very likely, a long stint in the Cyroki prison . . . if you're not hanged for the traitorous behavior that'll surface when this investigation begins. And I do hope, Decklin, I do so hope, that you haven't for one second, for one fucking moment, thought about trying to fuck me, because I swear I've already sown the seeds in my favor." Colms pulled another leaf of skachi out of his jacket pocket, rolled it up, lit it.

"You're a dirty bastard, Clay."

Colms puffed twice on the skachi. "How do you think we survive in this world, Captain? By doing whatever we have to. Now go do your fucking job before I pass this"—he slammed a finger on some parchment on the table—"up the chain and you lose everything."

"Fuck you, *cyr*." Royal slipped out of his chair, pushed it in against the desk so hard it pressed the table into Colms's stomach, ripped his medal off, and threw it at the lieutenant's face. The medal bounced off his face, leaving a red mark.

"Get. Out. *Now*."

When Royal was halfway out the door, he heard Colms call out, "And don't you come back until it's done!"

Fuck Colms.

Outside, Royal kicked a clump of snow. He paced back and forth, furious. He wasn't sure how much time passed, but it was a significant length. *I need to figure this out.*

Royal was no murderer. He'd killed before. He'd done

some things others would scoff at, sure. But to kill Sergeant Tekth? Seemed a bit out of the ordinary.

He could flee. *Flee to where?* Cyrok was a cold country year-round; he couldn't disappear into the wilderness and hike to the nearest town. He'd need passage on a ship to get to another country. As a convict, that'd be near impossible to achieve.

"Captain Hoarst," said a familiar voice. One Royal disdained.

He turned around and saw a man with a mustache—Blago Adavir—staring back at him.

"Adavir."

"Walk with me, please, Captain." Adavir's tongue darted out and across his mustache, a habit Royal noticed the first time he'd met the man.

Adavir led Royal away from the populated section of Coldridge.

"Where are we headed, Adavir?" Royal asked after they turned down a third alleyway.

"Just a bit farther, Captain. Don't want anyone to overhear us."

Adavir stopped behind an old stack of empty crates. "Captain, I'm told you're . . . resistant to current orders. I understand, I understand." He held his hands out and shook his head, like there was nothing he could do about it. "Orders are orders though." He retrieved a sheathed dagger from his belt. "This is your tool, cyr. Lieutenant Colms told me to give it to you. Oh, and this." He reached into a pocket and handed Royal a silver flask. "Finest whiskey. Lieutenant Colms said to tell you, 'finest whiskey in that flask to remind you what's at stake.'" Adavir licked his mustache, glancing up at the sky. "It's about to snow. I better get inside. Don't want my lips to chap." *Maybe stop licking them.* Adavir smiled, retreated down the alley, and left Royal to himself.

Royal looked at the dagger, the flask. Wanted to try the

alcohol, knew he'd fall down a rabbit hole if he did. Wanted to unsheathe the dagger, knew he'd fall into a fox den if he did. Either way, he'd break a leg. Instead, he put the items away and headed to the tavern, vowing to read the sign. He forgot, of course.

Although it was early evening, Royal sat and contemplated what to do at his normal table. No food, no drink, no distractions—other than the usual annoying occupants.

Reinkath entered the tavern not long after Royal and laughed when he noticed the captain. "And here I thought *I* had problems, Captain!"

Royal ignored the man, and Reinkath went about his carousing with his friends.

"You sure you don't want anything?" a server asked for the third time.

"No, I'll wait."

"As you say." *I've said it three times now.*

He'd decided to complete his mission that night. The longer he waited, the worse it would become. The more guilty he'd feel, the more nervous, the more self-hatred that would show. He had to get it out of the way. Finish the job. Get Colms off his back.

When Sergeant Tekth entered, he spotted Royal immediately and grinned. "Captain Royal, been wondering about where you were last night. Saw you at your thinking post— didn't want to bother ya. I've got all the guys calling you 'Royal' now, you're gonna love it." He laughed, sat, and waved the server over. "Start with the usual triple round, Captain?"

"Yeah, that'll work." Royal's hand slipped down into his pocket and grasped the hilt of the dagger Adavir had given him. He let go of it and placed his hands on the table, away from the weapon.

The server returned with their drinks, and Royal tipped one back as soon as she set the glass in front of him. Straight down the gullet. The back of his mouth roared in fury. Warmth descended through his body. He smacked his lips and licked his whiskers. No sense in wasting it. Wiped his mouth with his jacket.

"Mmm." Tekth smacked his lips in unison with Royal. "Nothing like a spot of whiskey to warm you up in Cyrok, eh?"

"Indeed, Sergeant, indeed."

"Something up, cyr? You seem off."

Royal waved him away, picked up a second drink. Tekth held his drink out to toast, and Royal obliged, glasses clinking before he tipped that one back too. Straight down the gullet. The back of his mouth roared in fury. Warmth descended through his body. He smacked his lips and licked his whiskers. No sense in wasting it. Wiped his mouth with his jacket.

Fuck Colms.

"So, Royal, you should stop by tomorrow, see the men. Can't be spending *all* your time alone in the office with Colms, huh?" Tekth laughed, drained his third shot.

Royal followed suit. Straight down the gullet. The back of his mouth roared in fury. Warmth descended through his body. He smacked his lips and licked his whiskers. No sense in wasting it. Wiped his mouth with his jacket.

That's enough alcohol. I can't do this drunk. "I got something for you, Tekth."

"Really, cyr?"

"Yes. Follow me."

"Yes, cyr!" Tekth hopped out of his chair and fell in step behind Royal.

Mother Avani, forgive what I'm about to do. As far as Royal could tell, Mother Avani was a tall tale meant to give people somebody to thank or somebody to curse, depending on the situation.

Royal led Sergeant Tekth through the alleyways Adavir had brought Royal hours earlier. It was getting dark and cold. Most people were inside. Assuming everything went to plan, nobody would hear anything.

"Just over here," Royal said, bringing Tekth to the stack of old crates.

"Why are we out here, cyr?"

Royal got behind the crates. "Over here, so nobody can see us."

"What've you got, Royal?"

Royal pulled out the flask Colms had given him. "Finest Cyroki whiskey, given to me by Colms himself. Didn't want anyone in the tavern to see it. It's just for us, Tekth."

Tekth held out his hand. Royal handed him the flask, then reached in his pocket, grabbed the knife hilt. *If I don't do this, I lose everything.* Not that Royal had anything to live for. But neither did Tekth.

Tekth tipped his head back, putting the flask to his lips.

And then it happened. Royal stabbed Tekth. Straight in the gullet. The blade went all the way through. The back of Tekth's throat ripped open. Royal retracted the dagger. Warm blood cascaded down Tekth's body. He stared at Royal, betrayal in his eyes, a tremble in his lips. Royal looked away, smacked his lips, licked his whiskers, couldn't find any alcohol, but there was a slight coppery taste. Some of Tekth. Blood gurgled out of the hole from the dagger. Royal wiped his mouth with his jacket. Noticed blood on the sleeve. Tekth choked, sputtered in surprise.

"I'm sorry, Tekth. Orders, you know?"

Tekth gasped, reached out at Royal, fell to his knees, and sputtered again.

Royal knelt next to the man. "I'm sorry," he said again. He drove the dagger into Tekth's chest.

Tekth blinked once, then collapsed.

Looking at his bloodsoaked hands, Royal fell, back against the crates. He stared at Tekth's lifeless body, blood draining into the alley. *Fuck Colms.*

A few moments of self-loathing and grief-ridden silence later, Royal collected his thoughts. He wiped his bloodied hands on Tekth's trousers, retrieved his flask—now stained red—and stood, leaving the dagger embedded in Tekth's body. Royal tossed the sheathe into the pooling blood.

He wiped the flask as clean as he could and walked back to his home.

It would take years, and lots of alcohol, to burn Tekth's empty from Royal's mind.

———

He slept. Not well and not much, but he slept.

He woke. Made himself proper. Cleaned what needed cleaning. Trimmed what needed trimming. Polished what needed polishing. He was missing his medal, though.

Royal marched to the barracks. Strangely, several Falcon Knights were outside. They didn't come to the barracks often, unless they were conducting official business, and that wasn't supposed to occur until the end of the week when Cyr Oxhorn was expected to arrive.

Inside, several more Falcon Knights had their hands on their sword hilts, calling out orders to various men. *My men.*

"Hey, what's going on?" Royal asked Marchessa.

"You didn't hear? Shit's going down. Oxhorn's in Lieutenant Colms's office."

He wrinkled his brow, confused, and approached the office. The door was open; he entered. Lieutenant Colms wasn't present, but Cyr Oxhorn was ruffling through various parchments. A Falcon Knight was going through his superior's desk. Royal now understood why Colms was so concerned before.

"Ah, Captain Decklin Hoarst, I presume?"

"That's me."

"Close the door, Captain." He did. "Take a seat." He did that too.

Cyr Oxhorn sat in the lieutenant's chair. She had clipped hair, near bald, and bits of metal imbedded in various parts of her face: lip, nose, ear. Dangles and bobs that Royal figured would hurt to be pulled out.

"Captain Decklin Hoarst, are you aware of what's transpired?" *A murder?*

"No, cyr."

"Lieutenant Clayton Colms has just been arrested."

"Why?"

"We've caught him pilfering money from the military's stores. Lining his pockets, among a variety of other crimes. He'll spend the rest of his life in prison, Captain."

A knock on the door, then it opened. "Cyr?"

Cyr Oxhorn looked annoyed for a moment. "Yes?"

"A citizen discovered a body. He's been identified as Sergeant Gamondo Tekth, one of Lieutenant Colms's men."

The body was just found? We're more incompetent here than I realized.

"I'll be right there."

"Cyr," the messenger said, and closed the door.

"You came earlier than expected, Cyr," Royal said.

"Yes, well, we wanted to catch Lieutenant Colms off guard. Any idea where Blago Adavir disappeared to? Reports suggest he stole a horse and fled town after we arrested Colms. Evidence suggests Adavir was assisting the lieutenant in criminal activity."

They were going to arrest Colms, anyway? Fuck. I've killed a man for nothing. Royal closed his eyes, leaned back in the chair. *Fuck.* He heard his heart thumping, felt the pit of his stomach jerk. "Fuck," he said. *Fuck Colms.*

"Captain, are you all right? You'll have a new lieutenant soon, I promise."

"I need a drink."

"You're sweating, Captain. You sure everything is all right?"

Royal wiped his forehead and unbuttoned the first couple buttons on his jacket. "I need a drink," he said again.

"Captain, why don't you take the rest of the day off? I know you were probably close to the lieutenant, but if this has affected you that much, you need some time."

"I don't care about the lieutenant, cyr. I knew Sergeant Tekth. Knew him very well."

"I'm sorry for your loss, Captain." Cyr Oxhorn retrieved a few coins, handed them over to Royal. "Go have a drink for yourself and a drink on your fallen comrade. He's served his country well." *Until I murdered him.*

"Thank you, cyr."

Cyr Oxhorn saluted him. He saluted back.

Dismissed for the day, Royal made his way back to the tavern.

He remembered to read the sign: The Disoriented Bachelor. Royal almost laughed at the irony.

Taking a spot at the table in the corner, he placed his feet on the table and waved over a server.

"I'll take three of my normal."

"All right."

"And three more. In Tekth's name."

"I'm sorry for your friend's—"

"Just bring me the drinks. And never mention his name to me again."

"Right away, Royal."

He snorted at that. The name had taken hold. *Because of Tekth.*

Royal drank the six shots in a row. Straight down the gullet. The back of his mouth roared in fury. Warmth descended through his body. He smacked his lips and licked his whiskers. No sense in wasting it. Wiped his mouth with his jacket.

He forgot the name of the tavern, and over time, he forgot about Tekth. He drowned himself in alcohol, sat at his table, alone.

He didn't mind being alone. It was safer that way.

What did one get out of companionship, anyway? Things that one feared to lose. And Royal didn't need those things. He had himself and his drink. For eight years, anyway.

Then, like things always did, Shit's Blessing hit him in the face when the war showed up.

CHILD OF CHILDREN

Her name was Ashen, likely because being born in black ashes will make you so. Between dirt, tattered clothes, and a lack of clean water, grimy layers cloaked her. But, as her father would say, "A good disguise buries lies." Her father had neglected to inform her the disguise didn't hide guilt, too.

At one time, they'd been happy. Ashen, her father Slade, and her mother Omari. They'd lived in a little nook between the city's walls and the back of a smithy.

She didn't have many memories of either parent, truth be told. Omari died when Ashen was four years old, assaulted and killed by a group of off-duty city guards. Slade died when Ashen was nine, murdered by an urchin over a heel of bread. *Guess I'm an urchin now.* Now she'd reached twelve, the same age her mother had been when Ashen arrived. For three years she'd survived the streets of Anepolis. A miracle, according to her best friend and companion, Spider, who she'd known for a few months. Life on the streets bonded you quicker, she figured. Ashen could only speculate, as she hadn't lived in a house before.

She was crouching, looking over a roof, examining the

cobblestone streets below. "Too crowded, still," she muttered, pushing herself away from the wall and sitting. She leaned against a pillar, watching Spider twist a small silver fork in his greasy hands. He never let go of it. "Well, ain't this a puppet show for dimwits?"

Spider ignored her insult. "Need ta git off this roof if we're ta eat t'night, Ash."

"Yeah. Anyone sees us and we can't return here."

Spider grunted. She wondered what his real name was. Probably he wondered what it was—he didn't remember it. Ashen had called him "Spider" because of his ability to scale buildings. He had long, lanky limbs and stringy, black hair, so the name fit, she figured.

"Could always go back ta—"

"We ain't going back to my parent's place!" And they wouldn't. Some other poor fool could live behind the smithy. *It's too crammed, anyway.* Least, that's what she told herself. Truth was, it reminded her of what she was missing out on. Family. "Could always sell the—"

"I ain't sellin' the fork!" It was a regular argument. Ashen's old home was the only other safe place they knew about. They needed more money, but the only thing of worth they owned was a piece of some poor noblemen's cutlery. A memento from Spider's past, allegedly. He claimed he'd been tossed out by a well-known family after giving them one day's lip too many, and the only thing he possessed to remember them was a silver fork. Ashen didn't believe it—if he couldn't remember his own name, she doubted he'd be capable of remembering his family.

"Then I guess we're picking," Ashen said. "Picking" was what she called "stealing", it just had a nicer ring to it.

"Aye, guess so." Spider pocketed the fork, pulled out a slimy cloth that was more snot than material, blew his nose, then put that back, too. She wondered how the inside of his ragged pocket fared, then thought better of exploring it.

"Where at?"

"Wherever we can git more than crumbs and scraps. I'm half a Starve, Ash." She didn't like the sound of that. According to Spider, Starves were people who finished off the hungry, consuming them—easy prey. Spider had recounted an attack he suffered by a tall, skinny man who shouted about being a Starve. She was sure she'd seen a Starve or two around herself, but she'd never gotten close to them. One thing for certain was she couldn't start eating other people. *Gross.* "Can't keep livin' like this." Spider grabbed his stomach and feigned fainting, though it wasn't far from where they were heading. They needed proper food soon—it'd been four days since they'd last eaten.

"Lemme check again," Ashen said. She crawled across the platform they sometimes slept on, a small square spot in-between two pillars and a sloping roof atop a church. A statue of a woman—their goddess, Mother Avani—took up a size-able chunk of the square, but several corners allowed Ashen, Spider, and their meager belongings to fit.

She peeked around the leg of the goddess—not a place Ashen thought she'd ever be—and peered down at the street again. Dozens of citizens strolled by, all well-fed and well-clothed. She growled her disgust, and her stomach rumbled back in agreement. Or, perhaps, hunger. Ashen returned to Spider's corner. "We have to go now. Ain't no way around it," she said. "Unless you want to wait until dark."

"No." He didn't have to elaborate. They'd both had little luck after dark. And, though neither of them voiced it, they found the night scary. Gangs and murderers emerged in darkness.

Her father, Slade, had left her an important piece of advice a few days before the urchin murdered him: "Never let them know you're a girl after dark." Slade referred to both Anepolis's guards and people who appeared when the sun set. "Both are dangerous and both will ruin you. Your mother knows better than anyone." She wished she could remember her mother. Ashen knew she had blue eyes, cute cheeks, and short fingers. All qualities Ashen possessed. All qualities her father said reminded him of her. Ashen wondered which of her qualities she'd gained from her father. Once, he'd said, "There isn't a bit of me in you, and yet, I love you more than anyone I've ever met." She hadn't known what he'd meant by that. Still didn't. And now he was gone. Choosing to honor his request, she sheared most of her hair off, and kept it short.

"All right, let's go," Spider said.

She considered gathering the few things she kept on the church's roof—a frayed blanket, a pair of bloody wool gloves, and a skin filled with smelly water—but hoped they'd be returning. Ashen's negligence at following her father's rules, one of which was, "Never assume you're returning to the last place you felt safe", might not've been the best decision upon reflection.

They waited a few moments for a break in the crowded streets, then dropped from the rooftop onto a strip of grass, separating the building from passing carriages and people.

A woman's shrill voice shrieked in surprise when they landed. "Vagrants! Summon the guard!"

"Time ta go, Ash!" Spider took off, running from the woman, who continued shouting and pointed at them.

Heads turned in their direction, and Ashen saw a nobleman attempting to unbutton his coat so he could free the hilt of a decorative saber he wore. *Useless fool.* Only somebody of incredible wealth would button their coat over their weapon. Ashen ran.

The shrill woman's cries of "Guards, guards!" followed them down the alley they turned into.

Spider hopped atop a stack of crates, pulled himself onto a low roof, and jumped a wall. He dropped a rope, which had been planted by some gang long ago, to Ashen, and she grabbed hold. With his aid, she hauled herself up and over.

"Thanks." She took a breath and examined their surroundings. They were one street away from the food stalls.

"No problem, Ash." He coiled the rope and threw it back on the wall. There were plenty of escape routes just like the one they'd used scattered around the city if you found them.

They skulked to the next street, prepared to run from any pursuing citizens or guards. When the market came into view, they stood, backs rigid, and walked as if they belonged, like any other citizen. Though dirty, they'd found that most citizens didn't question dirty people—there were plenty of normal citizens who had filthy occupations. As long as they didn't behave like thieves, people would, hopefully, ignore them. And, if they acted like they belonged, nobody questioned them.

This didn't mean vendors and guards weren't on the lookout. The market attracted dozens of gang members, thieves, and cutpurses. Beggars lined the outer perimeter, hoping to squeeze an extra coin from passersby—often with no luck. Ashen had attempted begging before. She found it rather despicable, because Anepolis's citizens weren't generous, preferring to insult and laugh at her. Ashen abandoned begging two days after her first attempt.

A decrepit-looking thin man in tattered rags, sitting among the beggars, stood and started ambling their way, cup clinking with coins in hand.

Ashen gasped, tugging at Spider, who noticed the man and hissed. "A Starve! Quick, inta the crowd!"

They melded with folk who, incredulously, didn't appear bothered by the Starve walking among them.

"Let's just git some food and git outta here," Spider said.

Ashen, afraid to even speak, just nodded.

They found themselves in front of Wenlick Banehorn's stall, which sold loaves of baked bread, hardtack, fresh and dried meats, wheels of cheeses, and apple tarts.

"Thank you, Mr. Banehorn," a customer said.

"Yepper, yepper. Anytime!"

"What can I do for you?" Wenlick asked her.

Ashen, caught up in the transaction, forgot herself for a moment. "Ain't sure, just… looking."

"Yepper, take your time," he said through closed teeth. His eyes narrowed, and he watched her, suspicious. *Do you recognize me?* Ashen had picked from him before, albeit many months ago. He'd caught a decent look of her face, too.

"My wife makes a good apple tart," Wenlick motioned towards the dessert. "And we bake our bread fresh, every day."

Spider, now in position behind the stall, gave her the signal—a single finger wiggling twice from around the corner.

"I would like—"

A shrill voice yelled through the crowd. "Vagrant!"

Ashen turned, saw the noblewoman who'd spotted her and Spider earlier. "Well, ain't that a shit dropped from a rat's ass?" Ashen said.

"Hey, you stole from me before!" Wenlick growled, retrieving a hatchet.

Wasting no time, Ashen bolted into crowded streets. She heard the clatter of boots behind her. She wished she had decent boots. Hers had holes, were a size too large, and stunk of rot inside. Ashen found the boots on a decomposing corpse a few weeks back—a homeless man who hadn't gotten enough to eat. *Or a Starve killed him.* Though, she realized while sprinting, he hadn't been eaten.

Ashen glanced over her shoulder, saw Spider lashing at a guardsman's calf with his knife, then ducking beneath an outstretched hand and disappearing into people. She turned the corner and slammed into something solid. Felt as though her ribs all shattered at once.

"My, my, are you all right?" A man wearing a golden-lined green cloak, with a decorated rapier on his belt, and a mustache hanging below his chin, bent over, a leather-enclosed hand reaching down to help her.

Another of her father's rules, "Never accept a helping hand," entered her mind. She pushed herself up, groaning at the throb in her side. "Ain't dead, so I think I'm okay."

"Splendid. Say, you look as if you could use—"

"No, I can't," she said.

"I'm Jaspard Couliac. Please, allow me to offer—"

"Thanks, but I need to go."

Jaspard frowned, hands on hips and turned his gaze to the pursuing guards.

Ashen had learned other things from her father, Slade, aside from his Five Rules of Survival. He'd taught her to watch for opportunities. To be impulsive when it mattered. Covering her mouth with one hand, she used the other to pull out a small, tightly wrapped bundle of Black Dust, and smash it into Jaspard's face—right beneath his nose. The contents sprayed into the air and Jaspard started sneezing and yelling, his eyes reddening.

She drew the elegant rapier from its scabbard and ran. The sound of Jaspard's sneezes followed her and the confused Anepolis soldiers stopped to aid Jaspard, forgetting their pursuit.

It was out of the question to return to the church roof. If followed, the Anepolis city guards would station themselves there for days, waiting for them to come down—or even worse, they'd find a way up. She'd lose everything she left behind. Ashen soured at this but brightened upon examining the beautiful engravings on Jaspard Couliac's rapier. The hilt, coated in gold, carved into a fierce-looking lion head. The steel blade, straighter than anything Ashen had ever seen, pointed to skewer, so polished she could see herself on the blade. "Well, ain't this rapier a piece of Mother Avani herself?" she said. It saddened her to think she was the reason it had parted from the scabbard. A sword this entrancing must have an impressive sheathe, she assumed.

Ashen sighed, looking around the stack of crates she sat behind, which created a small corner between two small houses that kept her hidden. It was her and Spider's prearranged rendezvous, if they ever split from one another.

She realized she was alone, and how odd it felt. Ashen hadn't been alone for several months, ever since Spider appeared, begging for a place to escape the chilly rain. Back then she'd holed up under a carriage which had lost a wheel. A temporary shelter, but one she'd claimed, nonetheless. She allowed Spider in, and they'd been together since. And now he was missing.

Not knowing what else to do, she recited her nightly prayer. "Never forgo food because it appears dissatisfying. Starving to death isn't worth it. Never accept a helping hand. You never know who you'll owe, and you have nothing to leverage. Never display your belongings, however meager they may seem. Somebody always has less than you. Never assume you're returning to the last place you felt safe. Unforeseen circumstances could mean you won't be able to. Never trust anyone, even those you trust. In matters of life and death, your life is meaningless even from your friend's point of view. Never let them know you're a girl after dark. Girls find themselves at the violent hands of angry men, and never leave them unscathed." All words reiterated by her father. All words she said, in her best impression of him.

A tear formed in her eye. Ashen blinked it out. She missed him. She loved him. Then he'd died. Another tear formed in the opposite eye. She sniffled, and then it was over. Ashen cried. And cried more.

Ashen spent the night cold and sad. She sniffled and cried, waiting for dawn. She was about to check other places when Spider showed.

"Aye, Ash," and Spider dropped from the crates.

"You're alive."

"Lookin' like you are, too." Spider handed her half a heel of wet bread. "I tripped. Dropped it into a puddle."

She took the soggy bread. "Well, ain't this a spread fit for a duck?"

"Careful o' the hunters, then, cause you're gonna be a duck."

"Never forgo food because it appears dissatisfying," she rehearsed.

"Aye."

Ashen bit into wet mush. Didn't even need to chew, just swallowed. "Gross."

"Aye," Spider said, again.

"You all right?"

He shrugged. "Close call."

"Sorry."

"Ain't your fault, I reckon."

"Still sorry."

"Thanks."

"Thanks for the bread." Ashen ate in silence, and, when finished, they left. She wasn't sure where they were heading and she knew he wasn't, either. They just started walking.

"Could go ta the sewers."

"Could kill me now," Ashen said. The sewer people were the strangest people she knew. And it was a dumping ground for bodies. "Starves probably live there."

Spider shivered. "Yeah."

"We'll find a spot."

Spider's eyes traveled to the roofs of the houses they passed. "Hope so."

"Preferably somewhere warm."

"Could go ta the home for children."

"Ain't going there. There are bedbugs. And dirty people with lice."

"We're dirty people, Ash."

"We don't have lice." She'd lied. Made her feel better.

Spider snorted. "Uh huh."

"What about the barracks?"

"On top o' the soldiers' barracks? Are you stupid?"

"Might not expect it," Ashen said.

Spider shook his head. "No. Absolutely not."

"Then where?"

He stopped. Pointed. "There."

She followed his finger to an enormous warehouse. Men traipsed back and forth, lugging huge sacks from building-to-carriage, or vice versa. "How are we getting inside?"

"Window."

She saw the window. Didn't see a way up to it. "You're crazy."

"I'm Spider."

Fair enough. She'd seen him climb wild things.

"We'll wait 'til evenin', then we'll slip inside and find a spot to sleep."

After the men on shift went home, the warehouse quieted. A single man stationed outside, sitting in a chair, and bouncing a loaded crossbow on his knee, was all who remained. He was easy to slip by once he nodded off.

It took Spider a few minutes, and he'd scaled the warehouse's side, hoisting himself through the window. Ashen inspected the wall, couldn't find a handhold. A few loose boards, a crack or two, nothing she'd consider climbing. Spider had a talent.

The rope dropped, and she grabbed ahold, bracing her feet against the wall. She climbed, and Spider helped pull her along. At the top, she collapsed, exhausted. "That took forever."

"Need ta get in shape."

"Not enough food to do that," she said.

"One day."

The warehouse's second story was crammed with sacks she'd seen the workers hauling earlier. She peeked inside—flour. Checked another—flour. It was all flour.

Spider shifted bags around, making a small lean-to. He sat inside it, grinning. "Not bad."

She mimicked his make-shift building and collapsed under it. "I need to sleep."

"Aye."

Ashen leaned the rapier against the sacks, then closed her eyes. She was asleep before she finished her prayer.

It was still dark when she opened her eyes, the only sound Spider's snores. Her thoughts drifted to her father. She wept every night since his death, but one detail stuck out. His murderer had severed a tendon below his knee. Even if he'd survived, he would've had an impossible time walking.

Nine-year-old Ashen waited all night for Slade to return home. He didn't. When she heard about the attack, she'd known in her heart it was her father who'd been the victim. Crying, she went to the barracks and asked what happened. Witnesses reported a young boy had seen Slade walking with fresh bread. The boy drew a small knife, ambushed Slade, and slashed his knee. After Slade fell, the boy flicked his knife across her father's throat. Her father choked to death on his own blood, while the boy escaped with the bread. It didn't seem worth it then; it didn't seem worth it now.

Ashen's mind wandered to the day before. Wenlick Bane-horn's stall. Freshly baked bread. Spider giving her the signal —a wiggled finger. A woman screeching. Guards approaching. She fled, caught a flash of Spider ducking and slashing at the same tendon.

She blinked. Darkness was still there. Spider's snoring the only sound. *It can't be.*

The circumstances around meeting Spider were strange. She'd left her home days after her father's death because she couldn't stomach living there anymore. She'd stayed in various places—a stint at the home for children went badly, she'd spent a few days near the sewers and became creeped out by its inhabitants, and everywhere else she found tended to be near gangs or have poor cover from the weather. And throughout it all, she recalled seeing a strange figure maneuvering around the roofs, as if… they were a spider.

And then, when Spider found her that day, under that carriage, she'd seen a flash of guilt. Or was it fear? She'd let him in, grateful for the company. They'd been together ever since. But something… something wasn't right. Ashen couldn't place it. She thought she could now. Spider killed her father.

She seethed. Betrayal by the only friend she had on the streets. Her father's life, ended for no reason. Pointlessly, really. She'd been *helping* her father's murderer and sleeping next to him. How she wasn't dead, too, was both a mystery and a miracle. She needed to fix things. Her heart thumped in her chest and she wondered if it would be loud enough to wake Spider. She heard the pulsing in her eardrums, felt her face go hot. She couldn't lie still anymore.

Ashen grit her teeth. *Should've known.* "Never trust anyone, even those you trust," her father said. Boy, had he been right. She climbed out of the flour sack house, gripped around in the dark for the rapier, took a step towards Spider's den, kicked a sack. The lean-to collapsed.

"What the—"

Ashen pressed the tip of the rapier down into Spider's body. She couldn't see where it was.

"You're killin' me!"

"Like you killed my father?"

Silence. Then, "Ash, lemme—"

She pushed harder. The tip bit into his flesh. He screamed.

"You killed my father over bread!"

"I was hungry! My ribs were pokin' out!"

"Well, ain't this an excuse of a politician?" She made coal of her heart. Then she drove her point home.

Spider gurgled, then ceased to move.

She twisted the rapier, just to make sure. He groaned, then loosed a last gasp. Spiders were stubborn that way, had to make sure they'd died.

"You fucking Starve," Ashen said. She let go of the rapier, heard it snapping back and forth, returned to bed. It wasn't yet light, and her exhaustion returned. This time, she said her prayer fully. "You're welcome, Daddy."

Ashen lacked the desire to return to thievery and scavenging. She wanted something different. An opportunity for a better life. And, after packing her stuff and leaving the warehouse at dawn, Ashen decided her next move.

Judging by the looks people she passed offered her, they didn't see many dirty children with fancy, unsheathed swords marching through the city. She worried they might call upon the guard, but where she was going, there'd probably be guards, anyway, so she didn't worry about it.

It made her nervous, even though she was optimistic about the plan. "Never forgo food because it appears dissatisfying. Never accept a helping hand." She chanted through the rules, clearing her mind. "Never display your belongings, however meager they may seem. Never assume you're returning to the last place you felt safe." She knew she was breaking several. "Never trust anyone, even those you trust.

Never let them know you're a girl after dark." Slade's Five Rules of Survival, rules she'd lived by, with a sixth added after his death. Rules she believed kept her safe, and now she was breaking them.

"Where are you going, boy?" a guard barked. She'd turned onto a road leading toward rich manors.

"I have a meeting."

"Who with?" The man approached, a sneer on his lips.

"Jaspard Couliac."

He shook his head and laughed. "No, you don't."

Ashen bit her lip. She wasn't sure what to do. Most of her life she'd been passive, reacting to situations rather than causing them, trying to prevent commotion and engagement. She didn't know if it was the comfort of the rapier in her hand, or maybe avenging her father by killing Spider, or perhaps she'd matured, but it didn't frighten her anymore to take matters into her own hands. Or, in this case, knee. She drove her leg into his cock.

The guard gasped, dropping.

Ashen grinned. "Well, ain't this a fortune turned upside its head? About time you bowed to someone like *me*." She slapped him across the cheek, then turned on her heel and strode away. After a moment, she picked up her pace. Ashen was braver, but not stupider. *Foolisher?* Stupider didn't sound right.

An iron gate surrounded Jaspard Couliac's manor. Normal people probably didn't know every rich person's house. Living on the street, you learned these things quick, learned who was who and who lived where on the off chance the information would be important one day—either for stealing or begging or learning who to avoid. She unlatched the gate, marched to the door, and tapped hard with the rapier's hilt.

A woman in plain clothes answered the door. "I believe you have the wrong home," she said, after a quick appraisal.

"I think not," Ashen said, holding up the rapier. "This belongs to your master."

"No one is my master, urchin." She started closing the door.

"Regardless, he'll want to have this back."

"You stole Lord Couliac's sword? The guard shall see you hanged."

Ashen's lip trembled. "I hope not." She hadn't thought her plan would fail.

Another woman arrived at the door. Her hair styled ostentatiously—a sign of her wealth. She wore silk clothes, complete with frills and folds. Jewelry seemed to flash on every part of her body.

"What's going on here?" the fancy lady asked.

"Lady Couliac, this urchin stole My Lord's sword."

"Well, invite her in. It would be unseemly if we allowed somebody to collapse from hunger in front of the house. She looks half-starved. He'll decide what to do with her."

Ashen blanched. "I-I-I'm not a Starve."

The plain woman looked confused. "A what?"

"I don't want to eat you," Ashen said.

Lady Couliac frowned. "I would hope not. Bethinda, please prepare something for this... girl?"

Ashen nodded.

The lady smiled. "Come inside."

Bethinda separated from them—Ashen assumed she went to the kitchens. Lady Couliac led her to a room with several chairs and not much else. Windows stretched the height of the room, looking out at the streets of Anepolis. A few people walked by, but this part of the city remained less trafficked than most.

Even being inside the mostly-empty room, Ashen stared at every detail. Everything was decorated with something or shined from polished metal or glass. Even the carpet was detailed and colorful and she didn't want to walk on it.

Ashen worried about touching anything, worried her dirty clothes, her dirty hands, would ruin everything they encountered. Awestruck, her mouth hung open as she gazed at Lady Couliac's wonderful dress. After a moment, Ashen realized she was staring, realized she needed a clean head, and forced herself to pick her jaw up and stop staring.

"Please, sit. Lord Couliac will be here shortly."

Ashen sat, cradling the rapier in her lap.

"Explain your concern about… eating me."

Ashen cleared her throat. She'd never talked to anyone about this, other than Spider. They'd shared the fear together, felt it unnecessary to mention whenever it could be avoided. "Spider, my friend—no, enemy—well, it doesn't matter. He's dead now. He told me about Starves. Monsters who feed off weak, hungry people, like me."

"I'm not sure what happened here, but there's no such thing as a Starve. To starve just means you're hungry."

Ashen didn't know whether to believe Lady Couliac, so she bit her tongue. She turned her head at approaching footsteps.

Jaspard Couliac entered the room, mustache gleaming with wax. His golden-lined green cloak trailed behind him, and he wore the rapier's scabbard at his belt, empty.

"Well, what a pleasant surprise," Jaspard said. "You brought back my sword." He reached into a pocket, drew out a small bag, and popped something yellow in his mouth. "Sugared honey chew?" he asked, extending one to her.

Ashen didn't know what that was, but, in the words of her father, "Never forgo food because it looks dissatisfying." She took the yellow blob and put it in her mouth. It was, by her memory, the sweetest thing she'd ever tasted.

"Let it melt for a bit, then chew it. Sticky, gets stuck to your teeth, but it tastes a dream," Jaspard said. "Allow me to introduce myself. I'm Lord Jaspard Couliac, and it seems you've met my cousin, Lady Alora Couliac, who's been vacationing here in our lovely city. What, may I ask, is your name?"

"Ashen."

"Before we get further into this conversation… what was it you smashed in my face?" Jaspard asked. He didn't seem angry, just curious.

"Black Dust," Ashen said. It'd been the first and only time she'd used it. "Somebody must've dropped it. Been saving it for the right moment." She swirled the chew in her mouth, bit into it. Sweetness popped in her mouth, and she swallowed. If this was any indicator of a rich lifestyle, it was better than she thought.

Alora leaned forward in her chair. "What's Black Dust?"

"Black pepper, red pepper, and sawdust. Supposed to make you sneeze. Hurt your eyes."

"It worked!" Jaspard pointed to his eyes, as if it still irritated them. "I felt like my face was about to fall off, but the effects didn't linger long. Lady Ashen, I see you have my sword. I can only surmise you're here to return it?"

"It's yours." Ashen held it out to him. He took the rapier, eager and pleased, sheathing it.

"Well, that was simple. Thank you."

"I was hoping you could help me," Ashen said.

Alora stood. "I'm sorry, but we don't have time for that. Bethinda will bring you something to eat, then you must go."

Jaspard spread his hands. "There's really nothing we can do for you."

"That sword's worth a lot of money. I brought it back. I'm just looking for… something. Anything. A job. Ain't nothing I won't do." She wasn't lying. If it would get Ashen off the streets, she'd do it. Anything.

"Neither of us is looking to adopt," Alora said. "We have nothing for you."

"Well, ain't this the will of the selfish? Come here in good faith, get shit on. It's no wonder everybody hates you. My father always said, 'never trust anyone, even those you trust'. Guess he was right."

The Lord and Lady glanced at one another.

"Perhaps he was right. We have prior engagements approaching," Alora said. "Farewell, Lady Ashen… what's your family name?"

Ashen had to think about it. Been so long since she'd used it, she'd almost forgotten. "Ashen Hyrel."

Jaspard Couliac beamed. Seemed she'd done something right, finally. "Hyrel? There's only one Hyrel family in Anepolis and they are part of the King's Council."

Ashen shrugged.

"You know, we might be able to make this work. Come, come." And he wrapped his arm around her shoulder, drawing her close. It felt nice to be accepted like that. "We have a lot to do, Ashen. Much work, indeed. You, my new friend, are going to be the ace in my pocket. We'll get you clean, sneak you on the inside. Show the true nobility what we think of them. Yes, yes… they'll never see it coming. And then you'll kill them." He laughed, eager. "You'll kill them all."

She'd do whatever he wanted if it meant a better life. Murder would be just fine. *Well, ain't this a way to end an urchin's story?*, she thought. Of course, it didn't turn out the way she hoped. But did it ever?

THE SAINT OF RIVANE

Saint Godfrey, they called him, though his name was the reverse, and he weren't so nice. Lord o' the Broken. Bastard Under the Bridge, though he knew who his parents were and hadn't stayed beneath a bridge in months. Remeria's Remorse. The King's Nuisance. But Saint Godfrey was the usual. The title they weren't afraid to say to his face.

Godfrey Saint rubbed his nose. Or what remained, anyway. Half had been dislodged because of an unfortunate duel years ago. His opponent, the woman, hadn't come out so lucky—he hadn't underestimated a woman since. Godfrey snorted, hawked, and spit a glob o' phlegm. Coughed, hawked up another bit, swirled it around with his tongue, chewing on it for good measure. He spat a second time. *Worthless.* Everything was worthless, and he was over it.

Godfrey smelled of dirt, sweat, and piss, which was much better than his sad regiment of men. "A'right you fuckers, hurry," he said. "Worthless, everyone o' ya."

"Be nicer," his second-in-command, Hershen, said. "Otherwise we'll lose more to desertion."

"We've already lost 'em to desertion, Hersh. Hardly gone anywheres and we've lost two. Two, Hersh. *Two.*"

"We don't want to lose more. We *can't* lose more."

Godfrey grunted. "Times are difficult. Leaving me'll end in ruin, for 'em."

"Sometimes they need to learn that for themselfs." Hersh shrugged and went to comfort the ragtag band o' ugly fucks who made up their group.

Godfrey didn't know what to call his merry band. Bandits? Mercenaries? Survivalists? Rebels? They belonged to no one, cared about no one, and were motivated by no one. They were vagrants. The homeless, ruffians, degenerates. A band o' brothers and sisters who'd drawn the short stick of shit during their lives. And now, with the Vessian invasion of the Camel Clans, Remeria, the country the town o' Rivane rested within was in a state o' panic, after being plundered, pillaged, and plowed through. Godfrey Saint despised the Remerian military for its lackluster defense, though he wouldn't offer his services. In fact, he'd dodged several attempts at being drafted. Same as the rest of the crew. Perhaps they'd call themselves the Remerian Runners.

He itched the missing side of his nose, always expecting to feel flesh where there wasn't any, and instead was greeted by jagged edges and scarred tissue. Godfrey gazed out at the meadow where his band camped. He met the eyes of a nasty-looking woman, replete with a dirty face and mangled claw of a hand—the result of her prior husband thrusting it into a cook fire. Gorsen was his name. Or was it Morsen? Godfrey didn't remember. The woman, Mauve, dipped her head in Godfrey's direction. He returned the nod and swiveled his eyes toward Rivane, the town they'd left that morning.

During a normal day's travel, they'd be out o' sight of Rivane. The group could clear many miles in a day; same as any healthy human could, but Mauve had forgotten her favorite belt, and Hershen wanted to steal more supplies, and the blacksmith's boy—Althier?—wanted to pilfer a sword from his father's smithy while he was out for lunch. So, against Godfrey's desire, they'd returned, which frustrated him. Then they'd spent far too long in the town, and by the time they'd left it was near dark. He'd considered calling off the whole traveling thing until the next day, but realized if he did, they'd never leave. There'd always be another excuse. Another reason not to go. So they'd left. And now, at dusk, they camped within sight of the town they'd abandoned twice in one day.

Godfrey gritted his teeth, grumbling to himself. Complaining wouldn't fix the issue, and at least they'd gone. He stared at Rivane, the town he hated, despised, thoroughly abhorred. The setting sun illuminated the small river which wound its way through the town. It'd take less than an hour to reach the damn place, that's how close they were. Godfrey spat, annoyed. He spotted the bridge he'd huddled under once in a storm. Lived there for several months because he'd gotten kicked out o' his own home. Never mind the fact he'd not paid taxes. Never mind the fact his wife had left him and his son had gone out and got hisself kicked dead in the head by a horse. Never mind the fact his asshole employer, Jeverrard Donik, had fired him and Godfrey hadn't been able to find another job.

"Lord o' the Broken, what are you thinkin' 'bout?"

He narrowed his eyes at the nickname, but recognized the voice and didn't reprimand her. Mauve had been married to a man who could do nothing better than yell. And hit. Godfrey knew a little more wouldn't phase her. "Just wishin' we'd got an earlier start, is all."

"Aye, 'twas me who'd ruined that plan." Mauve patted her belt. "Couldn't leave this jewel behind, ya know?"

Godfrey glanced at the frayed belt. In its center rested a rusted lion's head belt buckle. He grunted, not wanting to offend.

Mauve stuck her reddened claw out at him. "I know it ain't look like much, but I wear it as a 'minder 'bout the past."

"Your husband, ya mean."

"Aye, Morsen, the damned prick." She giggled. Godfrey knew why. After Morsen stuck Mauve's hand in the flames, she'd grabbed a pewter candlestick and rammed it into his testicles. Then she'd beaten him in the face with it, shouting and screaming louder than a cat in heat. When the local guard showed up, she was covered head-to-toe in Morsen's blood and still beating his body. Mauve had been a wealthy gal, never wanted for anything. Except a bit o' respect, maybe. She'd lost everything and claimed she'd never been happier. Godfrey weren't sure that was true, but didn't argue. Mauve had become a valuable asset and fit in well enough.

"Ya want some food?" she asked.

Godfrey grunted again. Didn't feel much like talking. Especially to her. Or Althier. Or Hershen, even. Anyone who'd delayed their escape from the town who'd rejected him.

"Me, Lord?"

He narrowed his eyes again. "I told ya not to call me that."

"Ya like Bastard Under the Bridge better?"

He clenched his jaw, grinding his teeth. A couple more weeks like this and he wouldn't have any teeth left.

"So, Lord o' the Broken it is."

"I should call ya Morsen's Murderess."

Mauve grinned. "Ya act like I wouldn't enjoy it."

Godfrey closed his eyes. *Have to keep it together, God. Have to lead your people to a better place.* Godfrey called himself "God" sometimes not because he felt he was a deity, but because nobody else had what it took to get things done. Only a superior being could conjure this rabble into something useful. Something that'd change things for the good and hardworking folk. *Get things done the proper way, that is.* If he was honest, Godfrey had an elevated opinion of himself. He knew he shared this attribute with plenty o' people in power—the same people he despised—so he kept it secret how he felt about himself.

"Fresh bread won't last past dawn," Mauve said.

Godfrey waved her away and she retreated. He admitted his surprise at the fact they still had fresh bread at all. He'd figured they would've eaten it on the first—and only—hour of travel they'd completed, such was the quality of idiots he marched with. *You get what you can afford.* Which was why they'd stolen everything they had, and he was leading a bunch o' entitled poor people. Not that he could say much. He was just as poor, though only a tenth as entitled, he figured. Given the right opportunity, he'd work. Least, that's what he told himself. Now it seemed too easy not to work— with the following he'd amassed, Godfrey figured he might start taking what he was owed.

"Aye, what are ya doin', dimwit?" Mauve shook her clawed hand at Althier, who looked confused. "That's our cook pot, not our washbasin, ya imbecile! Well, whatcha waitin' for? Pull your filthy fuckin' foot out, damn it! First night and ya wantin' to make us all sick? The fuck?" Her hand rattled back and forth in the air, pronged fingers-and-thumb contorted in the setting sunlight, like a pitchfork.

Godfrey shook his head. He'd get some food, get some rest, and then figure out what to do in the morning. But first, he needed to get away from these fools.

Saint Godfrey they called him, though his name was the reverse, and there weren't a lick o' religion within him. He would, however, be lying if he said the amount o' nicknames he'd gained didn't flatter him. And, upon self-reflection, Godfrey had decided Saint Godfrey weren't too bad a name. It had an air about it. A certain ebb and flow he enjoyed. He chuckled to himself. Ebb and flow? Now that's thinking like an educated man.

He'd slept a few hundred feet away from the group, with his own fire, his own space beneath the twinkling stars, and his own food. *Asides, plenty o' room for all of us in this field.*

"Saint Godfrey, how'd ya sleep?" Hershen asked, thumping over with heavy footsteps.

"Better'n you lot, I'm sure."

"Aye. Lots of complainin', but I'm sure ya—"

"Hersh, what do ya think about 'ebb and flow'?" Godfrey asked.

"Sounds like some shit a rich woman in silk might say when she gives herself a twirl."

Godfrey nodded. "I can't disagree."

"Why?"

"Just ponderin', is all."

"Ya sound like a man of clutcher."

Godfrey blinked. Surely Hershen weren't that foolish. "Culture."

"Aye, that's what I said. Clutcher. Git yer ears checked, Your Lordship."

"Get everyone ready. We're a leavin' when the first breeze chills my nose," Godfrey said.

"I don't know what that means."

"It's just a sayin'."

"Strange sayin', Godfrey."

"It's a new one. Just get the men ready."

"Aye!" Mauve's shrill voice echoed from behind Godfrey. "Who says I'm a man?"

Hershen left to get the bastards ready, while Mauve made her way over.

"It's endless, ain't it?" Godfrey asked himself, but knew Mauve heard.

"Nothin's endless, everythin's final," she said.

He squinted, trying to figure that one out. Itched his half-a-nose with his middle finger, peered at the rabble eating their morning meal, packing up supplies. Ultimately, he settled on a grunt.

"Not comin' up with a response?"

"Not a clever one," he said.

"Fair enough." Mauve pointed at the people with her claw. He knew she did this on purpose. Weren't afraid o' showing it to people. Considered it a trophy rather than a curse. "You got a group willin' to die for ya, Saint Godfrey. Times are a changin'. And it's good to be on top o' the change. But we need to figure some things out right about now, I figure. With the capital under siege, courtesy o' the Camel Clans, we have an opportunity."

Godfrey reached down, picked a dry piece o' stalk, and popped it between his teeth, chewing on it. A grassy, earth-tasting juice started forming in his mouth. "You've been with me since the start, Mauve."

"I'm not disputin' that, Lord o' the Broken."

"Can we stick to something a bit more favorable? Nobody's gonna want to be called the 'Broken'."

"I didn't think ya liked the King's Nuisance much. Or Remeria's Remorse."

"Perhaps we'll just stick with the familiar. Saint Godfrey."

"Aye, you want the peoples to worship ya, don'tcha?" Mauve pointed her three-fingered hand at him. "They're already doin' what ya want."

"They need something to believe in, Mauve."

"They's here, ain't they?"

"Something more than just 'being here'. We're all here. Something to look forward to. More than Hershen's empty head, or your wagglin' claw in the morning."

"Ya mean you."

"Well, if it motivates them…"

"Ya just tryin' to cement your legacy with a name."

"Is that upsetting?"

"No, but if you're gonna be Saint Godfrey, I want a name, too. Like ya said, I been around since the beginnin'."

"How about Red Mauve? Ya know, after… that." Godfrey pointed at her hand.

Mauve looked at her hand. "You wanna name things after body parts now? I'll be Red Mauve and you can be Bony Smallcock. How's that?"

"How can a cock be bony?"

"Does it matter? Ain't what ya want to be called, is it?"

Godfrey shook his head. "No, Mauve, it ain't."

"Wonderful. I don't want to be Red Mauve. What kind o' name is that? A color and my name? Pathetic. How about the Red Duchess?"

"So ya like 'red', eh? Ain't that name just a color and a title? Not much different from Red Mauve."

"Call me Red Mauve, and I call you Bony Smallcock."

"Point taken. How's about the Bloody Duchess?"

Mauve grinned and stuck her claw in the air. "Aye. I like that better, Saint Godfrey. I see great things for us, methinks."

"What about Hershen?"

"What about him?"

Saint Godfrey they called him, though his name was the reverse, and he weren't yet dead. Godfrey couldn't recall ever meeting or hearing of a Saint who hadn't already died and been forgotten by most. He'd be the exception, o' course. Aided by the Bloody Duchess, Saint Godfrey, and his group of Saintmaritans, as they started calling themselves—he hadn't had a say in that one—had marched for several days, subjugated a village, claimed plenty of loot and food, and overall, had very high morale. Bloody Duchess earned her moniker as she'd cut the throat of an unruly farmer's wife who wouldn't stop shrieking and bleating like the sheep in her pasture. They didn't kill the sheep, though. Well, aside from the two they took for food. Or was it three? Saint Godfrey weren't keeping track. That was Hershen's job.

In an hour or two, assuming Althier was correct, they'd come upon a small village called Riverwash or Wetgove or something. Back in the hamlet they'd already passed through, Beaver's Dam, the Saintmaritans had gotten their first taste o' victory, and a small smattering o' blood. Saint Godfrey antici- pated his flock becoming more zealous, more hungry for more war crimes. Couldn't say he blamed them. Remeria hadn't taken care of its civilians. *Fuck King Sedoa.* Alondo Sedoa, King o' Remeria. A blight on the land. A curse of man. Remeria's truest Remorse, Godfrey figured.

Saint Godfrey marched at the front of the Saintmaritans, brandishing his recently acquired hatchet, hacking away at various tall reeds and bushes. Weren't his favored weapon, but it was a weapon, and everyone knew they needed more o' those.

"I see it!" Althier said, pointing at the distant hamlet. "It's Rainclover! It's Rainclover!"

A cheer passed through the Saintmaritans upon hearing the news.

The Bloody Duchess and Hershen both made their way over to Saint Godfrey.

"What are ya thinkin'?" Hersh asked.

The Bloody Duchess—she refused to be called Mauve anymore—gestured with her claw toward Rainclover. "Aye, we subjugatin'? Killin'? Thieverin'? Could use a fair bit more recruitin', too, if'n you're lookin' to rule the lands."

"I'm not looking to rule. I just want a fair shake. Enough food and money to last is all I please. But the kings and queens and dukes and duchesses all wanna hoard it for themselves."

"Aye, but not this one," the Bloody Duchess stabbed herself in the chest with her marred thumb. "I believe in sharin'. Problem is that the people with everythin' don't. Sometime methinks we should kills 'em all. Time to show 'em how pleasin' to the heart it can be. To share, that is. With us."

"Ya can't just make 'em share, Beedy," Saint Godfrey said.

"Beedy? The fuck ya sayin'?"

"Shortenin' your name. It's a long title. Gets repetitious-like."

"If I wanted a short name, I woulda picked a short name, ya know? When ya address me, use my proper name. Otherwise, no point in havin' it, wouldn't ya agree, Saint?"

"A'right, I get it, Bloody Duchess," Saint Godfrey said. *For God's sake, there have to be rational people out there who can become reliable officers.*

Just then, a cheery song started, encouraged by Althier:

"We're the Saintmaritans,
We're the Saintmaritans!
Led by Saint Godfrey, the king'll be sorry,
It's time to claim our stake!
Follow the Bloody Duchess, the only noble who's like us,
She'll help remove the fake!

We're the Saintmaritans,
We're the Saintmaritans!
Saint Godfrey is lovely, he'll start recovery,
Time to bring down the king!
Loyal and un-royal, we're about to get joyful,
As we'll take over by spring!

We may not be the smartest, gonna try our hardest,
We vow to march the furthest!
We'll kill our ungrateful king!

We're sick, we're tired, we're old and inspired,
Remeria's gettin' retired!
We'll kill our ungrateful king!"

A loud cheer came from the rebels.

Saint Godfrey held his hand up for silence. The Saintmaritans quieted. He knew this weren't because they respected him—they only trusted him this far because they'd found food, money, and victory—but he enjoyed the illusion. "Saintmaritans, we've conquered a hamlet." He smiled, itched his half-nose, held his hand up for silence again. "This here's village'll have more supplies. We're taking everythin' we can get our hands on—food, weapons, clothing, people. Aye, that's right. We need recruits if we're to kill a king." Another round of cheers. "Fuckers have been robbin' us blind all our lives. It's time we put a stop to it. Time we had a voice! It's time Remeria freed itself from nobility. Whatever happened to charity? Whatever happened to equality? We're gonna take it all and redistribute it! Show 'em nobles how it feels to be us!"

The crowd hooted in agreement.

"You tell 'em, Saint Godfrey!"

"We'll piss on the king's face!"

"I want 'nuff to feed my children *and* me's wife!"

Althier thrust his father's sword into the air. "We're with ya, Saint Godfrey! We're with ya all the way!" More cheers of agreement, though Saint Godfrey weren't sure he believed 'em. Thought it was more so the hype than reality. He grinned regardless o' what he thought.

The Saintmaritans continued their march toward Rainclover.

Hersh shook his head. "They're a happy now, but wait 'til things don't go as well."

"Ain't gonna happen, Hershen," the Bloody Duchess said. She pulled a knife out with her good hand, pointed it at Rainclover. "Good thing's're about to occur. A legend'll be born today."

She was correct.

Saint Godfrey they called him, though his name was the reverse, and he was beginning to embrace the change. He weren't upset watchin' the Saintmaritans waltz into Rainclover like they owned the place. A buck-toothed, cock-eyed peasant greeted them at the fence gate surroundin' the small village.

"Greetings, neighbors! Where are you coming from?"

The Bloody Duchess was first to approach Bucktooth. "Here to appraise the goods!" And just like that, the Bloody Duchess drove her knife into Bucktooth's stomach. Ripping the blade sideways, she spilled his innards. Then, to Saint Godfrey's amazement and disgust, the Bloody Duchess reached inside the screamin' Bucktooth with her claw and pulled out a handful o' muck. Cackling with glee, she raised her bloodied and withered hand above her, lettin' the gore drip and spatter down her face and chest. Not missin' a beat, the Bloody Duchess slit Bucktooth's neck wide open and kept on stomping and hollerin' into Rainclover, clawed hand contorting and dancin' in the air above her the entire way.

"We're gonna have to have a talk with her, ain't we, Hersh?" Saint Godfrey asked, turning to Hersh. But Hershen weren't there. He'd joined the crowd and ran on in, crowbar lifted high, ready to kill.

"Surround by idiots, o' course," Saint Godfrey muttered, but he gripped his hatchet tighter in his fist and followed the Saintmaritans.

It took a few moments for the people o' Rainclover to figure out what was happenin'. By then the rebels had already slaughtered a dozen of 'em.

Saint Godfrey turned the corner of a small hut, saw a woman crouched in the building's shadow. He grimaced. *Ain't no kindness in rebellion, though.* "Got anythin' useful?" He cleared his throat, embarrassed. Saint Godfrey had forgotten his manners. "Ma'am?"

The woman shuddered and bellowed out a cry.

Ain't gettin' anything outta her. Saint Godfrey sighed and dropped the hatchet into her forehead. *Specially not now.*

Blood and glory. That's what they wanted, that's what they got. The Saintmaritans killed half the village before the good people had enough sense to scream "I surrender!", so they didn't harm 'em. They were only civilians, after all. That was an unwritten rule for the Saintmaritans. Saint Godfrey had spoken it once, though.

"And who might ya be called?" the Bloody Duchess asked a groveling man on his knees. He stared at her feet like he might dip down and give 'em a kiss.

"Bartlesby, My Lady. Bartlesby Flatchett."

"What an awful name," she said. Then she reached down with her claw, hooked his chin with that mangled forefinger, and turned his head up so she could stare him in the eyes. "Bartlesby Flatchett, ya says?"

"Yes, yes, My Lady. Please don't hurt me. I have children." Bartlesby paused. "At least, I did a few minutes ago."

"Are you accusin' us o' murderin' children, Bartlesby?" the Bloody Duchess asked.

"Nope, no ma'am. Never." He gulped, swiveled his eyes around. Caught nothin' but other Saintmaritans starin' at him.

"Why don't you grab what you want and leave? Bartlesby's never hurt a fly, you ugly cunt!" One o' the other subdued men had stood, givin' the Bloody Duchess a sneer. "You're just murderers, gonna kill us all, anyway. So make it faster, and get it on, you cold bitch!"

Althier hopped over to the yeller and, at sword point,

forced him up to the Bloody Duchess. "Here ya go," Althier said, kickin' the man's leg and pushin' him to the ground.

The Bloody Duchess pointed her withered finger at him. "State your name, pig."

"Sashton. Leave us alone or kill us faster, but this isn't right. I know your accent. You're from that stupid town to the south, you're—"

The Bloody Duchess's blade found its way buried in Sashton's throat. He reached up, grabbed the hilt and weren't able to do anything 'bout it, cause the Bloody Duchess's boot had kicked the knife before Sashton could pull it out. Sashton gurgled once, twice, then keeled over.

The Bloody Duchess retrieved the blade, wiping the blood off on her chest. "Anyone else have somethin' to say? Nay? Good. I believe our esteemed leader would have a few words." She gestured in Saint Godfrey's direction.

He nodded his thanks to the Bloody Duchess, still feelin' a bit o' shock regarding her sudden savagery.

"I'm Saint Godfrey, and this is my crew—the Saintmaritans—weren't my choice, but that's what they wanted, and that's what they are. No changin' it, I think. We're not murderers, though I confess, might've overindulged when we entered this village. I suspect an apology wouldn't go over well, so I won't make ya suffer the sad attempt. I will say another thing or two, though."

Saint Godfrey took a moment to look each one o' the captured citizens in the eye, then continued speaking. "The king o' this country has run it like shit for the last several decades. We're sick of it and we're goin' to his city. We're goin' to stake our claim. King Sedoa won't continue to sit on the throne. We're gonna kill 'em. And when we do, we're gonna share his gold-plated blankets and silver encrusted fruit. We're gonna give away thousands o' gems and keep many more for ourselves. It's time we take what's owed us—call it interest on what's been stolen. I ain't askin' any o' you to join us. We just murdered many you called friends and family. I get it. If I were one o' ya, I'd probably have stood up like poor Sashton over there."

Saint Godfrey glanced at Sashton's body, lying in a puddle o' blood. He noticed the Bloody Duchess swirling a bare toe in it. He returned his attention to the prisoners. "I'd've gotten killed, too. Hothead, I used to be. Stupid, too. Now? Probably a stupid hothead. I'm just more careful where I aim it. King Sedoa's preoccupied defendin' the country from the invading Camel Clans. Which means it's the perfect opportunity for us to gather some troops and go take advantage of the chaos. It's true—I killed some o' you. We all did. We're takin' most o' your money and food, too. But consider this: if you come with us, if ya fight against the people who really deserve it, ya might end up better off. Ya might end up rich."

A few joined them. A few remained defiant, like Sashton, and ended up at the wrong end o' a blade. It weren't personal, just business. Saint Godfrey ordered others freed to spread the words and deeds of the Saintmaritans.

Saint Godfrey they called him, though his name was the reverse, and he now preferred the legend he was nourishin'. His band, the Saintmaritans, swelled to round forty-five people. Several had mentioned they'd heard tales spun o' what the Saintmaritans wanted to accomplish. One had even called Saint Godfrey a true saint come to save 'em all. Some o' the new recruits were bitter, sure, some might've even come along with the goal o' guttin' him in his sleep. He'd have to change things round—no more sleepin' by his lonesome, he figured. It was time to establish an inner circle. He'd call 'em the Originals.

Before they'd left Rainclover, Saint Godfrey gathered the

people who'd left the town o' Rivane with him while the new recruits prepared to leave their home for good.

"Listen here and listen good. We're a growin' unit and a growin' unit needs established leadership, methinks. So here's the deal. Everyone o' ya who left Rivane with me is now called an Original. Nobody can take that status from ya. We're the ones who began this, we're the ones who're gonna see it through. But with bein' an Original comes responsibility. We need to protect one another, aye? Keep us safe at night. Who knows who'll end up in our group, a marchin' with us? Legends are created with names, and a name I've got. Bloody Duchess got one, too." The Originals cheered.

"Aye. But with names comes problems. A lot o' problems. I propose we create an inner circle, protected by Originals. If you watch our backs, we'll watch yours, and the lot o' us'll see this plan through 'til the end. And when King Sedoa's body rests under one o' our boots, we'll disband the Originals and go back to the way things used to be. No leaders, no hierarchy, just a fair distribution o' the wealth and power." No one made a sound, so he wasn't sure how this was going over. He'd move forward, knowing full well they'd appreciate the next part.

"Organizations need leaders. Hershen has been my right-hand man since we left. Aye, probably longer than that, even. But times're a changin', and now he's gonna be in charge o' security. Captain o' the guard type deal, ya know." Saint Godfrey glanced over at Hersh, who stared at him, open-mouthed. *Can't please everyone. Sorry, Hersh.* "Meanin', we need a new second in command. The Bloody Duchess sounds a right candidate, eh?" A loud cheer for the Bloody Duchess.

She walked over to Saint Godfrey, beamin' and raisin' that reddened claw in the air the way she liked to. At her hip, her hand rested on the hilt of a stiletto she'd robbed someone of. "Thank ye, Saint Godfrey," she said. "I won't forget this." She wiped a tear which formed in the corner o' her eye. Or she faked it. He couldn't tell, but he appreciated the gesture.

More specifics were ironed out later. Saint Godfrey apologized to Hersh and also made it known Hersh was the only person he trusted to watch his back. He also promoted Althier to a captain, as well. The boy—really, Althier weren't quite a man yet—had a solid grip on the Saintmaritans, and Saint Godfrey knew this'd keep 'em better in check. Bartlesby Flatchett became the man in charge o' introducin' how things went to fresh recruits. He took to callin' himself the "quartermaster" on account o' makin' sure they had what they needed.

The Bloody Duchess took to her new role with a passion. She'd found a felt hat somewhere, with a wide brim, and wore it at an angle so she could still peer at everyone as easy as before. She'd also found a red cape she'd fashioned from a blanket or sheet or somethin', Saint Godfrey weren't sure. One thing's for sure, though, the Bloody Duchess looked a leader. She'd disappeared a few moments before the Saintmaritans were to leave Rainclover behind, delayin' them by an hour at least, just to find these costume elements. Saint Godfrey weren't pleased, but the crowd cheered for her, so he let it go.

Then, the forty-five men and women of the Saintmaritans left Rainclover behind.

Saint Godfrey they called him, though his name was the reverse, and he was beginning to feel like a sidekick to a god after all—so well-liked and respected the Bloody Duchess had become. Things were lookin' good. They passed through two more hamlets, near doublin' in size, though causin' Saint Godfrey to feel paranoid that one of the newcomers were loyal to the king. The Saintmaritans argued some, fought a little, but the Originals kept 'em together. Captain Althier taught the new recruits the Saintmaritan Ballad they'd continued to sing. Meanwhile, the Bloody Duchess just needed to walk by and tip her hat, swirl her red cape, draw her stiletto, or grasp the air with her mangled claw, and the people went wild. Saint Godfrey weren't lyin' if he said he'd become a tad jealous.

Hersh sang under his breath as he marched, though nobody else was singin'. Song stuck in his head, must be. "We're sick, we're tired, we're old and inspired, Remeria's I' retired! We'll kill our ungrateful king!"

"Captain Hersh," Saint Godfrey said.

"Saint Godfrey. Men are lookin' good. March is goin' swell. Few more days, and we'll be at the capital. Then what're we gonna do?"

"We're gonna figure a way to kill the king, o' course." Saint Godfrey hadn't figured out how yet. There'd be a way. He'd find one.

"There's a few other small towns between here and the capital. The Bloody Duchess is hopeful we can recruit some more from 'em."

Saint Godfrey furrowed his brow. He didn't like the Bloody Duchess talkin' about what *she* was hopin' for. "What about what I'm hopin' for, Hersh?"

"Didn't those thoughts come from your head? I figured what the Bloody Duchess wanted, ya wanted. Don't ya want more people to help? Can't bring down a king alone, I 'spect."

"Yes, Hersh, I want more help. I'm just worried, is all."

"Y'gettin' paranoid, Saint Godfrey. I swears, we're all with ya. At least the Originals are."

"Aye, monitor anyone you think is suspicious, Hersh. I don't want any loyalists to the king marchin' with us, ya know?"

"Always," Hersh said.

At midday, they reached Beauty in the Bay, a village

constructed in the bend o' the river which split Remeria in half. O' course, the town's name were debated in Remeria because, accordin' to educated folk, bays weren't in rivers. If they were, the bay would be at the end o' the river.

The Saintmaritans pushed their way into the village, disarming and gutting a few guards, before the villagers submitted to the takeover.

The Bloody Duchess took control over the proceedin's, o' course.

"We're the Saintmaritans, and we're here for a reason," she said. She did that thing where she put her claw on display. Let the prisoners see she'd been deformed. Let 'em see she didn't give no shits 'bout what they thought. She was the Bloody Duchess, didn't need no sympathy. "We're gonna kill King Sedoa, and we're gonna redistribute wealth and power to those o' us who've suffered." She went on to proclaim their plans. Saint Godfrey's plans.

He stood in the middle of the crowd and sulked. Everyone cheered for the Bloody Duchess. *Ain't like I didn't think o' all this first, though, eh?*

The moment the Bloody Duchess led the Saintmaritans out of Beauty in the Bay was the moment Saint Godfrey realized he'd lost control.

Saint Godfrey they called him, though his name was the reverse, and he weren't in command no more. He knew it, Captains Hersh and Althier knew it, and the bloody Bloody Duchess knew it. Since the four o' them shared a large tent, things'd gotten awkward. The captains took their orders from the Bloody Duchess and Saint Godfrey. They weren't sure who to listen to. The Bloody Duchess asked Saint Godfrey questions, a ruse to continue makin' him believe he was in charge. But he knew she knew he knew he wasn't.

Saint Godfrey might not've been the smartest man. He'd never claimed to be. He wasn't ignorant, though. Which was why he asked the Bloody Duchess to a private meetin'.

"Ya wanted to see me, Saint Godfrey?" the Bloody Duchess asked.

"Aye. I think we both know why."

The Bloody Duchess had the decency to look embarrassed.

"The way these things go often ends with somebody dead," Saint Godfrey said. "Meanin' a conflict o' leadership between two people."

"I ain't lookin' to kill ya, Godfrey."

"And I ain't lookin' to kill ya either, Mauve. But it's time to face facts. They respect ya more'n me. I'm gonna step down. Let ya take charge."

"I can't let ya go, Godfrey. Your name's started this whole mess. Can't do it alone."

"I never said I'm leavin', ya daft whore. I'm stayin'—as your second."

Saint Godfrey they called him, though his name was the reverse, and he weren't the reason the Saintmaritans were remembered. But he helped. And people would remember his name. Almost as much as Mauve's.

And so began the Bloody Duchess's legend.

BROOMS

ching joints, early mornings, grounds to clean, people to order about, check the power source. This was life. Ashmount, a university dedicated to teaching and studying magic, still needed maintenance; and Corzi Buttercork, better known as the Janitor of Repetition, the Normal in the Unnatural, or the Monotonous Motherling—monikers she'd come up with herself, of course—was the janitor. Nobody paid her much attention. Repetition, monotony, boredom. She had to entertain herself.

Aching joints, early mornings, grounds to clean, people to order about, check the power source. Corzi Buttercork was a woman of routines, diligence, and schedules. Never a minute late or early. On time. Never excited, happy, or energized—just completing another day, another hour, another minute in the repetitious, monotonous, boring life.

Aching joints, early mornings, grounds to clean—*oh look, a coin!*—people to order about, check the power source. Head janitor. She had a title, and her staff obeyed her. If she had issues, she went to one of the mages, or Wielders of Power, as she called them. Corzi Buttercork had only done that once with a helper she'd had long ago, and he'd disappeared.

Dead? Alive? Imprisoned? Who knew? It was almost more excitement than Corzi knew what to do with.

On this morning, Corzi started the day the same as every other. And finished it the same, too. Nothing was different, aside from the young boy shadowing her. A new hire.

"Corzi Buttercork is my name, but you'll call me Ms. Buttercork, or Ma'am. Don't want to hear any of the 'Corzi' shit, you hear? That's the name I call myself, and I call myself that name enough. Like some variation, though. Not that I'm all that old, mind you. Fifty-two isn't old. It's just not young, you hear? Of course you hear, you're eight. Are you paying attention, boy? Hey!" she said, snapping her fingers. "That's right, you pay attention. Next time you gaze off like that, I'll pinch your cheek. Corzi's fingernails are harder than iron, so I've been told. Don't want to feel them, I assure you. Make sure you soak up this knowledge, boy. Corzi doesn't play with safety here."

The boy, mouth half agape, followed her, nodding at the correct times and smiling when she asked him a question. She wondered if he was a mute, as he never answered her.

"We'll start with the first point—personal health. Corzi, in her ever-aging vessel, has aching joints. Hard work wears the body down, so we have to do something about it, boy." Corzi took a seat on a bench. They were underground, in the basement of Ashmount, near the supply closets. She spent most of her life under the earth. Couldn't complain. Sun was hot and bright. The boy sat next to her. "While I respect the need to rest, there's a task you need to fix your-self upon." She rolled her long dress up, exposing her pale calves, leathery knees, then handed the boy a jar of oint-ment. "Corzi needs that spread on her ankles, then her knees. Rub some life into them, boy, keep them awake. Going to need some rejuvenation if Corzi's showing you the way of things. Long workday ahead." She ahem'd, hoping to moisten her drying throat. Too much speech caused issues for Old Corzi, though she wasn't old. She just wasn't young.

This broke protocol. Corzi Buttercork, on a normal day, wouldn't sit and allow a boy to rub her arthritis-ridden joints. Today was special, though, as it was her birthday. She'd be a few minutes late because she wanted to be a few minutes late. Seeing as she was her own boss, she could do that. In actuality, Corzi had a boss. He was a Magicus, a mage who taught at Ashmount, and never paid Corzi any attention.

She sighed as the boy rubbed the ointment in, providing near immediate relief. "Good job, boy, now get Corzi's second leg." Once finished, she took the jar back. "Now let's make you a learned boy, or I'll have to answer to the Magicai. One word of advice, and Corzi never offers bad advice: Don't disobey the wielders of power, or they'll do something to you. Not sure what, so don't ask Old Corzi, but I can tell you they disappear. Dead, alive, imprisoned, I know not, so don't be asking Corzi." As an afterthought she added, "And I'm not old. I'm just not young." She stood, cleared her scratchy throat, and brought the boy to the employee storage room.

Half the room possessed expected amenities: cubby holes for employees to store their belongings, benches to sit upon, a changing stall for privacy. The other half stored various cleaning supplies, tools, and a shelf of vials holding a magic substance the Wielders of Power used. She didn't know how they got it, what else they used it for, or what exactly it did. Corzi just knew of its importance. Six brooms, propped against walls, wore various employee uniforms and a different hat perched on top.

"Sit," Corzi said to the boy, pointing to a bench. She clasped her hands behind her back and started pacing, employees lined up behind her. "Today's goals are the same as yesterday's and tomorrow's. We have a new employee," she gestured to the boy, who looked confused. "What's your name, boy? Corzi has a difficult time remembering. Not an age thing, always had a foggy memory. One day you'll understand. Don't look all confused on me now, I was only told your name the one time, if I even received that courtesy, and there are many of us walking these halls. Right, Elmon?" Corzi lowered her voice, "Yes, Ma'am!"

The boy frowned, but he uttered his name. Corzi didn't quite hear it, but she didn't want to ask him to repeat it.

"Nice to meet you, boy. Now everyone introduce yourselves—not you, though, Norax, you talk too much." She increased her speed and pitch, "Hello, I'm Ginnie, the resident hall sweeper, but my friends call me Gin. I think we'll become favorite friends!" She changed her voice to a crackle, and slow. So slow. "Mr. Marcs is my name, son, and you remind me of my cousin, rest his soul. I'll be happy to show you the ropes. Been here twice as long as the brilliant Ms. Buttercork, but I'm half as talented." Now came the tough part. Corzi cleared her throat, started almost yelling, so loud was the voice of Stoia, the camel rider. "Me Stoia, Great Warrior." Corzi coughed. "I murder and pillage, then become good man! Listen, Ms. Buttercork so smart, she!" Corzi quieted her voice, started whispering. "When I was young, I burned my throat. Inhaled the flames of a campfire. My apologies, but you'll have to lean in to hear me. They call me the Silly Silent, but my true name is Numara." Then, because Norax couldn't resist himself, Corzi changed her tone to a sinister snarl. "I won't let that Corzi bitch keep me quiet—no, not the great Norax. It was I who should've become boss here, but instead, Corzi's clever wile and sly dealings maneuvered her way up the chain! Together, perhaps, we could usurp her tyrannical rule!"

The boy, confusion etched across his face, had allowed his mouth to hang open. He said nothing, though that didn't seem unusual. Corzi wondered if she'd been given another simpleton to work with. *Between the schemers and the incompetence, I near have to do everything myself! Old Corzi doesn't have the body for this anymore, no. Not old, though, just not young.* She flickered her gaze back to Norax, the nasty pig. Who knew what Norax was planning anymore?

One day, I'll take you down, Corzi. And I'll use that boy to do it, Norax thought.

Corzi growled. She could feel Norax plotting against her.

The boy stared at Corzi. He appeared frightened.

"Aw, don't worry, boy," Corzi said. She hobbled over, sat on the bench next to him, resting an arm around the his shoulders. "You see, Corzi knows who each of these employees are. Been around them long enough, I could tell you each of their habits. For example, when you eat your meals, keep watch over Silly Silent. Might be she's hungry enough she'll steal off your plate. Sneaky shit, she is. Corzi's had more than her fair share of stolen food, I'd say. Might be Corzi's age—she's not old, mind you, she's just not young. Say, why don't we assign this motley crew some jobs? Then I can show you our routine."

The boy nodded. Corzi squeezed him against her for a moment. Almost like having her daughter back. Almost.

"Time to give these fools their jobs, Corzi thinks. "Elmon and Mr. Marcs, you'll both team up today and clean the dormitories on the first floor. Stoia and Ginnie will take the second, and Silly Silent will take the third." Corzi turned to the boy. "She's good enough to handle a floor by herself." Corzi shifted her gaze to the employees, all standing at attention, waiting for her to dismiss them. She saw Norax, eyes flickering back and forth, like he was trying to escape notice. "Aw, shit, we didn't assign Norax. You almost got away without a job today, Norax, but Corzi didn't let it happen. Not today! Old Corzi sure isn't old, she's just—"

Corzi changed her voice to the snarling one and interrupted herself. "Not old—how many times are we gonna hear that? And why do you always forget about me until last, you old hag? Every day's the same thing, same jobs. You ever gonna mix it up? Every time you forget about me, every time you put me on the school's grounds—with you! Well, you know what? I'm sick of it, Corzi Buttercork!"

Corzi narrowed her eyes at Norax. "You'll do what Corzi says, and you'll damn well enjoy it! They put Corzi in charge for a reason, and if any of you lazy sops feel like arguing about it, you can approach the Wielders of Power yourselves. Now, we have a guest, and we're going to show him what to do. No more of this fighting on his first day. It's not fair. And if the Wielders of Power find out we're sitting here yapping all day, they'll probably melt us all into puddles, so let's stop dawdling. Corzi isn't stupid. She knows powerful people dispose of assets that aren't helpful, including citizens just trying to make a living. Old Corzi knows a thing or two. She's not old, but she sure isn't young." Corzi took the boy's hand. "Come on, boy, Corzi's going to show you around. Follow along, Norax, or I'll break you in half like I did Tillary." Corzi's eyes darted to a corner where a broken broom lay.

The boy and other employees followed Corzi out of the basement and up onto the first floor. She took Norax and the boy outside into the grounds. "One rule when you're not in the basement, boy," Corzi said. "Keep quiet and don't lock eyes with any of the Wielders. Corzi's survived a long time by keeping to herself. If you prefer living, heed her advice."

The boy nodded, eyes wide. He was clearly frightened.

Norax snarled, and Corzi adopted Norax's voice. "Don't worry, boy, just stick close to me," Norax said, patting the boy's head.

Corzi glared at Norax, but stayed quiet—a group of Wielders were near.

Corzi and Norax showed the boy what needed doing: they planted new flowers and trees from seeds stocked in the basement; spread small amounts of food for the birds; trimmed plants and grass; cleaned up trash; polished the shiny parts of the building—doorknobs, windows, and any other decorations; and maintained the statue of their goddess, Mother Avani, which stood in the center of the grounds, facing a bridge leading out of Ashmount.

Norax inhabited Corzi's head for a moment with a few thoughts about that. *Back towards civilization. Back towards freedom.* But the freedom was many, many miles away, and Norax knew he couldn't escape. He didn't have the money. Corzi scoffed. Norax was always dreaming about other places.

"Look up, boy," Corzi said. Above them, a sweeping bubble encased the entire school and its grounds. "Protecting us from that." She pointed at a volcano spewing lava. Chunks of magma smashed into the shield, spraying rubble everywhere. Liquid lava spattered it, then ran in rivulets, draining into the lava moat which surrounded the building, protecting them from unwanted visitors. "We're safe here, but it sure gets lonely sometimes."

A Wielder of Power got close, and Corzi quieted, looking down in subservience. In truth, a Wielder had never harmed her, never said a bad thing to her, or any of her employees. It was just the knowledge of what they *could* do if they wanted that kept her and her people silent. He didn't bother them, and they continued working.

They met back in the basement, this time in the break room, for the midday meal. The other employees claimed they'd made good progress in their work. Corzi wasn't sure she believed them, but since she was training a new hire, she wouldn't be checking on them today. The boy needed Corzi's focus.

"Here you go, boy," Corzi said, setting a plate of food in front of him. She hoped he liked salted fish sandwiches slathered in lard.

The boy sniffed, and Corzi rubbed her nose with her finger realizing her nose tickled, too.

"It's not poisonous, boy." Corzi took a bite, closed her eyes as she chewed. She'd always taken the time to enjoy her breaks. Corzi worked hard, especially at her age—not that she was old, she just wasn't young—and it gave her time to relax her aching joints.

She noticed the boy staring at his plate, confused. A giggle came from the other side of the table. Silly Silent had stolen half the boy's sandwich.

"Really, Numara? On the boy's first day? He's young and needs his food, damn it," Corzi said.

Corzi, whispered in her Silly Silent voice, said, "I'm famished—you assign me an entire floor every day."

"Only because you work well! If everyone else worked half as hard as you, Numara—I'm sorry, Silly Silent—I'd be in charge of the entire school."

After they'd finished their meal, the employees returned to work. Corzi assigned Norax to help Silly Silent finish. She needed to be alone with the boy now. This was the most important part of the day.

"Excuse me," Corzi said in the low Elmon voice as he bumped into her.

"Typical, getting in Corzi's way. After you," she said, waving him by. Elmon was the first employee Corzi had hired. She didn't see him much anymore, didn't talk to him. They'd never had the best relationship. Thinking on it, she realized she'd forgotten most of his personality, wondered where it disappeared to. "Come on, boy. At least *you* have manners."

The boy shrugged, and Corzi led them to the storage room. She pointed at the shelf stocked with vials. "That, boy, is our lifeblood." Corzi lifted a vial, shook it in front of the boy's face. "This protects the school. It's the power for the shield. Magic powering magic—don't ask me how it functions, I just work here," she said, noticing the boy's confusion.

Corzi brought the boy to the power room. The room didn't have an official name. Or she'd never been told its official name. Or she had been told, but she'd forgotten. *No. Impossible. Old Corzi's not old, she just wasn't young. Plenty of time for her to lose her memory.*

Inside the power room, six tubes ran into a large box. They funneled the liquid out to six evenly spaced spots on the bubble shield. Corzi didn't know how it worked, just knew they had to be filled. "Today's the fourth tube," she said. Corzi unstoppered the vial and poured the liquid down the tube. "I do one a day, and take the seventh day off. When Corzi first started working here, she was taught to do all six at once. Shield needs power once a week. 'Mother Avani, help me', Corzi says to her boss, 'there's no way I can remember to do this once a week'. 'Well, aren't that too bad?' her boss said, poor grammar and all. Her boss then told her she'd have to get used to it. But Old Corzi, she's a wise one. After one week of getting yelled at for forgetting to magic the tubes, Corzi staggered the vials, did one per day. Guess the shield weakened during that time, but nobody noticed." Corzi giggled. "Nope, nobody noticed, and now, Corzi remembers—every day, except the seventh day, which she takes off, because everyone deserves a break."

The boy's head tilted to one side.

"Oh, dear. Corzi's boring you. Well, come along, boy. We're off to get ourselves supper—and end the workday early, Corzi thinks. You look exhausted, and if you look half as tired as Corzi feels, we could both fill our stomachs and then pass out. Being a janitor isn't easy. I would know, as I've done it for thirty-three years, but Corzi does it in the name of safety. This way, boy," she steered the boy around, as he'd been walking in the wrong direction. "You know, you talk very little for one your age."

The boy nodded.

"We'll have to change that, boy, as Old Corzi talks to herself a bit too much, could use some company. You've seen the fools I have to talk to around here. Nothing fun about any of the employees, but they get the job done, and they're nice enough folk, I suppose."

After they'd eaten their supper, Corzi realized she hadn't prepared for a new employee, much less one this young—the new employees would normally get their own rooms, but she figured the boy would be scared alone. He was only eight years old. "You can have my bed, boy. I'll sleep on the floor— no, I insist, it's all right. Corzi can manage. She'll pull out a few extra blankets, make a lump on the floor, curl up like a bitch about to have pups. It's comfortable, I swear. Well, it's not, it'll break my back, but you need a good rest after all this newness. Here," she helped the boy into bed, then pulled the covers up to his shoulders. "Rest well, boy." She leaned in, about to kiss his forehead, realized he wasn't her dead daughter, and pulled back, deciding to give him a friendly pat on the cheek instead.

Come morning—after stretching out her stiff back—Corzi fed the boy, helped him wash, then they were back to work. She led him to the employee storage room, where, for the second day in a row, she was last to arrive.

"Well, good job being on time, everyone." Corzi looked at Mr. Marcs, who'd been having problems lately. "For two days you've on time, too. It's almost a miracle. Perhaps Corzi should request a new employee every week—you'll always be on time, then!"

Mr. Marcs chuckled. Corzi slowed her voice, letting it crackle, and said as Mr. Marcs, "Not all of us have your time management, but that's why you're the boss, isn't it?"

"Damn straight," Corzi said. "Now, boy, today we're gonna—did you hear that?"

"Me no hear nothing," Corzi yelled in Stoia's voice. "Me never—"

The building rumbled. The boy winced, closing his eyes.

"Now, now," Corzi said, patting the boy's shoulder.

The wall behind the employees exploded, and a big stone chunk took the head off Silly Silent. Then a blaze burst through the hole, consuming the others.

Time slowed. Corzi yelled, grabbed the boy and shoved him to the ground. She lay on top, shielding him. *Why aren't the Magicai stopping this?* The wave of heat burned as it filled the room. The boy screamed, said something, for once. "I don't want to die!"

Corzi peeked out the corner of her eye, saw the explosion crossing the room. "Huh. I thought I'd do more," she said before the inferno incinerated her. The last thing she felt was the boy's hard wooden nose against her chin.

Less than a second later, the broom she'd been protecting burned up, too.

BLOODY GUMS

Family dinner happened to be two things: required and uncomfortable. This didn't change on a day-to-day basis.

"You're disgusting, Tythus," said Khlaux who was sitting across the table and sticking his tongue out, making an ugly face. One reason Tythus didn't like dinner was the constant berating he endured from his two siblings.

Tythus looked to their grandmother—the second reason he disliked it—expecting her to reprimand his older brother. When it didn't come, he asked, "What?", while a forkful of potato mash hung in the air, halfway to his mouth.

Khlaux laughed. "You have something in your teeth." Their younger brother, Elizer, remained silent, a grin stretching his cheeks.

Their grandmother scolded them, a finger pointed at Khlaux, and then Tythus. "Be quiet and finish your meal. I've had enough of this shit. Corbéo's have manners."

Tythus almost protested but knew he'd end up on the wrong side of a lashing. *Even though I've done nothing wrong.* Self-conscious, he felt around his teeth with his tongue, searching for whatever Khlaux had spotted. A string of fatty meat dangled from a crevice. *This is the last time I eat beef.* It was an empty promise. Tythus loved all meat. Except fish.

He pulled at the chunk with his tongue and it broke, half remaining between his teeth. Tythus almost moaned in frustration but didn't want to attract his grandmother's attention. He couldn't use his fingernail, either, because she'd get annoyed at the improper manners. Her reprimand played itself in his mind: *Corbéo's don't put their fingers in their mouths!* Then he noticed the knife. *Can't bitch about cutlery in one's mouth.* Picking up the blade, he started poking the crack, scraping downward to lure the meat out.

His hand slipped, and the knife tore open his gum. Wincing, he dropped it and gasped.

"Damn it, Tythus." His grandmother stood, slamming her fork onto her plate. "All you had to do was eat your food, but instead, you're slashing open your mouth."

Blood dribbled down his chin. He groaned—it hurt.

"A knife in the gums… what's next, Tythus? A fork in the ass?" His grandmother exited the dining hall, the door slamming shut behind her.

"You're an idiot, Tythus," his younger brother, Elizer, said.

Sniffling, Tythus excused himself and went to bed. He was nine, and it wasn't the last time he'd hurt his gums with a knife.

***

Their grandmother, Lady Elisi Corbéo, had become strict since their fourth sibling, Grist, had died. Sickness had taken him mere months after the mysterious deaths of their parents. Living with their grandmother had become a necessity, lest they want to live as urchins on the streets. She wouldn't've allowed that. The Corbéo's were one of Lochwall's most esteemed noble families, and their grandmother would rather die than become exposed to such scandal. The fact she had deep coffers didn't hurt anything, either.

Though privileged, Tythus felt he'd suffered a tough upbringing. His parents attended the nobility's functions. He didn't know what they did, but their lives had ended too soon, and his grandmother wouldn't discuss the matter. Then Grist passed. And Tythus had to deal with constant teasing from his two brothers. Even though *he* was older than Elizer. Somehow, Khlaux had roped Elizer in, left Tythus on the outs. So, he spent much of his time alone.

Now thirteen years old, his grandmother had given him a weekly stipend to spend, or save, as he wished. He'd saved every coin he earned, found, or stolen, stashing sacks in odd places around the Corbéo manor. Sometimes he'd sneak into one of his brother's rooms and pilfer a coin or two from their own stashes—they weren't so careful about concealing them —and add them to his own savings. It's not like his siblings deserved anything less; they'd bullied him for years and he was over it. He'd decided he was going to leave, but first, he needed enough money. Tythus saved for months, and when he wasn't studying, doing chores— "for discipline", his grandmother would say—or completing any of his other obligations or expectations, Tythus explored the city of Lochwall.

His grandmother wouldn't let him go alone, so sometimes he accompanied his brothers, or, more likely, he'd tag along with Lyron Surtz, one of the Corbéo's servants.

"Tskah," the servant made the customary sound he'd always made to catch the attention of whomever he was addressing. "Return at this location before sundown, sir." Surtz held his hand out, expectant.

Tythus deposited the required coin—a small payment to free himself from the servant and explore Lochwall unattended—and hurried to escape Surtz's sight. As long as Tythus returned to Surtz on time, the servant wouldn't question Tythus or alert his grandmother about his absence. He knew Surtz would turn him in if he caused any issues at the Corbéo home, though, so he made it his duty to ensure Surtz was happy with the arrangement—and paid—every time Tythus left. On a normal week, he could escape into the city, alone, at least once. At first, he'd explored different shops and restaurants, spent time in inns and taverns, and searched the slums— "An area nobility avoids," his grandmother would always say.

After a few weeks of exploration, he'd become enamored. Tythus had found his calling. A shoddy inn, sitting between the commoners' housing and the outskirts of the slums, and hardly more respectable than the beggars who graced the alleys nearby, Tythus met the mercenary, Ailose.

Part of a company called Legends of Lochwall, Ailose was —according to himself—the youngest member to get recruited in the organization's history. Considering Ailose was nineteen years of age, Tythus didn't believe him.

"Aye, T!"

Tythus smiled and wormed his way through the tables and patrons of the inn—Black Brew.

"Well met, Ailose."

The man smiled, drained the rest of his ale, and slapped the table in front of him. "Take a seat, let's hear what's going on."

Tythus complied and sat across from his friend.

"Already gotchu a drink," Ailose said, gesturing at the fruit juice.

"Thanks." Tythus took a drink and wondered what fruit somebody had turned into something so sour. He didn't like it, but it was part of the commoner's life, and he wanted to fit in. Although Black Brew didn't care enough to inquire about an unattended child wandering around, they wouldn't serve him alcohol. He'd inquired the first few times he'd come here.

"What's new, T?" Ailose always called him 'T'. After

Tythus had disclosed his identity to Ailose, he'd sworn the man to secrecy. Ailose knew about Tythus's desire to flee his family—had even offered to help him find a new life as a mercenary. But becoming a mercenary would mean remaining in the city, working as a Legend of Lochwall. The risk of being discovered by his grandmother was too great. He needed to escape the city altogether.

"Nothing. I don't have much time."

"Out with your nursemaid again?" Ailose laughed, refilled his mug of ale from a larger tankard.

Tythus laughed along with the mercenary. "I don't think you could find somebody less nurturing than Surtz." Then, after a moment's pause, "Well, my grandmother, perhaps."

Ailose lifted his mug. "I'll drink to that," and took a long swallow.

Tythus stared into his fruit juice, wondering what ale tasted like.

"So, T, you have 'nuff money yet?"

"I'd like more. Another year's worth, at least."

Ailose spluttered. "Another year? T, if I'd've known that I wouldn't keep hanging 'round here, waiting for you."

Tythus frowned. He couldn't lose Ailose or he'd never be free. "I need to get away."

"So, run."

"You don't understand my grandmother. She'd never let me get out peacefully. I need the money."

"I have me own work that needs doing, T. I can't keep waiting."

"I'm not asking you to sit around, not working. Keep doing your jobs, but don't die. And don't leave. Here," Tythus retrieved a small pouch of coins he carried whenever he ventured into the city, "take this as a retainer." He slid the pouch across the table. "You know the word, 'retainer', right?"

"I'mma mercenary, not a idiot. I'm paid on retainer often."

"'*An* idiot', Ailose."

"Yeah, I know…" he trailed off, took another swig of ale, then retrieved the money. "Thanks. I'll help you when you're ready to leave."

"I appreciate it, Ailose. Thank you."

"You're welcome. Now take a drink, lean back, enjoy the surroundings. Watch the women, eh?" He winked.

Tythus picked up his fruit juice, peered into it. "What's in this shit?"

Chuckling, Ailose took the cup of juice and upended it over the floor. "Shit, I guess. I don't drink the stuff. Here." He refilled the cup with ale. "Don't tell your granny I let you try this."

Tythus picked up the ale, sniffed it, took a drink, coughed. "That's strong." He blinked a few times, surprised at the overpowering flavor.

"Aye. You get used to it."

"I don't mind it." Tythus wasn't sure if he was lying or telling the truth. He took another drink of the ale. "Not as bad as the juice." Wasn't sure if that was true, either.

The remaining afternoon Tythus spent learning to enjoy ale; watching scantily clad women serve food and drink, while sometimes disappearing in the backroom with a patron, or once, there were two patrons; discussing his future with Ailose; and mourning his return to his grandmother's home. He kept careful watch out the front window, and, when the sky darkened, said farewell to the mercenary, then returned to Surtz, who led him home without a reproachful word.

About a year later, he'd almost saved his financial goal. After finishing a recitation of the Vessian Incursion, and the battles that took place—notably the leadership of the famous Remerian Lieutenant Caius Bonovak—to his tutor,

Tythus found himself outside the Corbéo manor. His older brother, Khlaux, sparred against one of the house's guardsmen and he'd become quite skilled with a blade. Their other brother, Elizer, was observing the battle, humming a tune to himself.

"You ever going to take up the sword, Eli?"

Elizer shook his head. "No. Fighting isn't for me."

"What is it you plan to do, if not fight?" Tythus had sparred fewer times than his older brother, but he still enjoyed the art. The guards praised his ability to adapt, though whenever Tythus fought Khlaux, he got angry if Tythus ever pulled off a successful trick. Khlaux, being older by a few years, bested Tythus nearly every time, but Tythus enjoyed angering his brother when he could; it made up for all the harsh words.

"I want to explore the world," Elizer said.

"Journey without knowing how to hold a sword? You're mad. You'll get yourself killed."

"I'll hire a guide. Or bring some of our guards."

"And what would you do while exploring the world, Elizer?"

"I don't know. Investigate different taverns. Listen to different songs. I like a fun song." Elizer started humming again.

Tythus grunted. "I think you'll find tavern songs a bit of a disappointment." He remembered the songs he'd heard in Black Brew. Though humorous, none of them would likely impress Elizer. Or perhaps they would. He couldn't say he knew his younger brother all that well.

"Perhaps the world needs somebody to create better ones."

"You?" Tythus laughed. "Wait until grandmother hears that."

Elizer's cheeks flushed. "Don't say anything."

He smiled. He wouldn't unless Elizer gave him cause to.

"Ack!" The guardsman sparring with Khlaux lay on his back, Khlaux's wooden sword tip at his neck. "You got me."

The door to the manor opened. "Tskah. It's time to wash yourselves." Surtz ushered them inside. "Best hurry," he said, "your grandmother's in a foul mood."

After cleaning themselves up, the three Corbéo boys took their seats. Their grandmother was already sitting at the head of the table and Surtz was pouring drinks.

"Sit. Be quiet. No misbehaving," their grandmother said, her now routine line whenever they ate a meal together. Her stern eyes flickered between the trio before leaning back in her chair and sighing.

Surtz poured Tythus some wine—his grandmother allowed the boys a single glass at dinner—before exiting to retrieve their first course.

They ate in silence. First, a bowl of egg soup. The clinking of silver spoons in pewter bowls broken up by the sound of a drink being sipped, but no discussion. Second, some roasted boar, complete with boiled carrots. Quiet again, though Elizer earned a reproachful stare from their grandmother after issuing a loud belch. Third, Surtz served a delicious, sugared cherry tart. Tythus found himself smacking his lips before he finished the first bite. After dessert, Tythus picked up a knife and used it to clear the food from his teeth. Despite the injury he'd sustained when he was younger, and the plenty of additional ones since, he found he preferred the pain of a cut gum instead of the odd feeling of something jammed in his teeth. He had to do it with caution, though, or his grandmother would lecture him. "We have picks for that," she'd screech. But he didn't think they worked as well as the tip of a knife. Or maybe he just liked the feeling of holding a knife, sticking something dangerous in his mouth. He didn't know.

When Surtz had cleared the dishes, their grandmother leaned forward in her chair and eyed each of them after clearing her throat. She was about to say something important, it seemed.

"I'm to be out of the manor for a few days," she said. "Business meetings. You'll be on your best behavior."

The three of them nodded.

"I mean it."

They nodded again.

"If I hear *one* issue, the three of you will face severe punishment."

Again, they nodded. Silent. Afraid of being yelled at.

"You may talk."

They asked questions simultaneously.

"Where are you going?"

"What are you doing?"

"Why won't you return home?"

Their grandmother held her hand up, quieting them. "Boys, you know I don't discuss my work. If you need anything, Surtz will take care of it. You'll learn more about the business when you reach adulthood. Until then, focus on your studies."

Khlaux and Elizer peppered their grandmother with questions, but Tythus tuned them out. He thought about all the free time he was about to have. With their grandmother gone longer than a few hours, perhaps he'd be able to escape. He'd need to pay Ailose a visit. First thing, however, was making sure he could bribe Surtz to let him out of the manor.

His grandmother was gone by the time Tythus washed and dressed himself the next morning. Khlaux and Elizer were both absent from the morning meal, which Tythus ate by himself. He'd offered a chair to Surtz, who declined, saying, "Why who, then, would serve us, My Lord?" Tythus hadn't an answer. Later, it occurred to him they could've served themselves.

After finishing his food, he waited for Surtz to finish clearing the table.

"Why are you still here, my lord? You have things to do."

"I need to leave, Surtz."

Surtz cleared his throat. "I think not."

"Please? I have something I need to do."

"Nothing is more important than your education." After a moment, Surtz grimaced and whispered loud enough for Tythus to hear, "Or my life."

"What do you mean?"

"I mean, my lord, that if your grandmother found out I let you into the city, alone, she'd flay me alive. I'm too young to die, sir." Surtz didn't look too young to die. But, Tythus admitted, neither did most adults.

"I'll pay extra." Tythus had been expecting to spend extra money and had saved some aside for this reason.

"Very good, my lord. Do return before sunset, please. If Lady Corbéo sends somebody to check on you boys, I'd like to prove you're all in a suitable form. And home."

"No problem." Tythus retrieved some coin from a hidden stash, paid Surtz—triple what he normally would—and, making sure he had a significant portion of money on him, left the Corbéo manor on foot.

He visited several stores and purchased a few odds and ends. If Tythus was to escape the Corbéo residence, and the reach of his grandmother, he'd need to get as far away as he could, fast. He bought a large leather bag, a fresh pair of boots, several traveling outfits, a cloak, flint, a brilliant set of throwing knives, and a pair of longer knives he kept in his belt, though he knew he'd have to hide them before returning home. Already, on his way to Black Brew, he was picking at his teeth with one of them. Wasn't sure why, there wasn't anything in them. He hadn't realized he'd been doing it until he'd poked a hole in his gums and the pain brought him out of his wandering thoughts.

After regaining his senses, Tythus continued walking in the inn's direction. He looked around and saw a man staring at him. When he realized that the man had been examining *him*, he returned his gaze to where the man had been but nobody was there. After he reached Black Brew, he glanced over his shoulder and spotted a figure in robes ducking down an alleyway. Unnerved, he entered and cleared his mind. Black Brew was livelier than usual.

Dancers spun and twirled on a raised stage. Patrons hooted and hollered, and a few were led out back, after money exchanged hands, of course. More servers than Tythus had seen before maneuvered through the throng of customers, pouring drinks, and delivering food. One side of the building had been cleared, and a man sang while three or four other people played instruments. A few of the lines made their way to his ears:

"Oh!
The lass would like a lay!
Whaddya say, whaddya say,
The lass would like a lay!
Give her strong cock and shiny new coins,
She'll find ways to moisten your loins!
Oh!
The lass would like a lay!
Whaddya say, whaddya say,
The lass would like a lay!
What's the trick, what's the trick,
To bedding a damsel who'll pleasure your prick?"

The noise stunned Tythus for a few moments, but he smiled and charged forward, spotting Ailose at the bar.

"Ailose!" Tythus clapped the man on the back, like he assumed any mercenary would do.

Ailose lurched forward, spilling his drink. "You bastard,

who the fuck— Oh, T. Hey. You ruined me drink." He frowned, then shrugged. "Weren't thirsty, anyway."

"Here, I'll buy you a new one."

"Great, I'm parched, T."

Tythus frowned. "You're drunk."

"Ain't drunk." He stood, wobbled a moment, then sat back down. "I'm a bit groggy, is all." He reached for the empty glass he'd spilled and tried taking a swig, set the glass back down. "Nah, you're right. I *am* drunk."

The bartender walked past. "Another round, Ailose?"

"Yeah," Tythus said, sliding a few coins across the counter. "And one more for me."

"Sure thing," the bartender said, scooping up the money. He poured a drink for Tythus, refilled Ailose's, and moved on to the next customer.

"Thanks, T."

They clinked glasses and downed their drinks. Tythus almost vomited, but he kept it down. He'd get used to it. It was time he grew up.

"I'm ready, Ailose."

"To be with a lady?" Ailose laughed. "There're plenty of 'em here!"

Tythus examined the room. It was more crowded than before. People continued coming but never seemed to leave. His heart skipped a beat. In the corner, a figure in black robes sat alone at a table, facing Tythus and Ailose. Tythus pretended not to notice and turned back to the mercenary, ignoring the fact the man looked like the one he'd seen outside. "What's the deal today, anyway? It's so busy."

"Yeh. It's music day. People come ta music day. Girls dance and fuck... half off."

"Oh, makes sense."

"Damn straight, T."

"I'm ready, Ailose," he said again. He wasn't sure why he

was delaying it. Maybe verbalizing it would make it permanent.

"Ready for what?"

"To leave Lochwall. I've got money."

"Eh?" Ailose's eyes followed a skinny girl wearing a shorter skirt than Tythus thought would be appropriate in a public setting. She led a patron to the back, and Ailose turned his gaze back to Tythus.

"I've got the money. To leave."

"Finally! Good job, T. I figured you were yanking me knob the entire time."

"No. Can we meet somewhere tomorrow? I brought coin with me today and spent it on these things," he gestured to his new bag.

"Meet me in the alleyway behind the tailor."

"There are like five tailors in the city."

"There're like fifty. Just five that you nobles use. The one across from Elph's, the leatherworker. Not so far from here."

"I know the place. I'll see you tomorrow. Just before dusk?"

"Aye."

"Good night, Ailose."

"Night, T."

Tythus exited Black Brew and made his way home. He couldn't shake the feeling someone was following him, but he didn't spot anyone. It was dark, though, and, thinking about the person he'd seen disappearing down an alleyway earlier, he knew someone wearing black clothing would be difficult to spot.

Tythus collected all his necessities and packaged them together. He went around the manor, unearthing his hidden money, pooling it in his room, though he hid it in his bag, and didn't leave its sight. Which meant his brothers and Surtz inquired why he was hauling the bag around the house, to which he replied, "I'm cleaning." His brothers just looked at him as if he'd lost his mind.

Surtz, however, had a different answer. "That's my job. Your grandmother *pays* me to do these things."

Tythus handed Surtz a couple of coins. "Just let it lie."

"Of course, my lord." Surtz beamed and pocketed the coin.

Once Tythus had his affairs in order, he delivered another significant sum to Surtz, but not before storing half his remaining money under his bed. He hoped his brothers and Surtz would stay out of there for the few hours he'd be out.

Tythus made his way to Elph's, the leatherworker, crossed the street, and found the tailor. Glancing around and watching for people in black robes, he made his way down the alleyway, where he found Ailose pacing back and forth.

"Aye, T, you made it on time."

"Ailose. I have the money you need."

"Wonderful." Ailose pulled out a flask, took a swig. "Want some?"

"No, thanks. When can we leave?"

"Tomorrow evenin', I can be ready."

"That works for me. We can meet here again if you prefer."

"Sure, T. Sure."

"Ailose, if you show up tomorrow, I'll double your money."

Ailose's mouth opened. "Wha?"

"I'll double your money. Consider it insurance." Truth be told, Tythus didn't trust the mercenary. He'd been saving double the money Ailose had requested for this very reason. If Ailose betrayed Tythus, he didn't think he'd be able to escape Lochwall.

"T, you don't have to. I'm not gonna fuck ya."

"I believe you." He didn't. "But I like you. You've been good to me." Mostly Ailose had gotten drunk whenever Tythus came around. "Nobody else can help me." Untrue. But that would mean finding somebody else who was willing, and he'd worked on Ailose for a year now.

"I'll be here. You can count on it. I should go, T. Get every-thing ready. We're gonna be on the road a long time."

"All right. Same time tomorrow?"

"Aye."

Ailose departed the opposite end of the alleyway as him. Tythus swore he saw a shadow dance above him, crossing a rooftop, but when he surveyed the area, he saw nothing.

He returned home to the Corbéo manor for one last night. Tythus wasn't a sentimental person and he knew he wouldn't miss his family. His grandmother was a shrewd, mean lady who couldn't give a damn about Tythus or his brothers. And, thinking about his brothers, he realized he didn't care about them at all. Khlaux and Elizer had ganged up on him since he was younger. He didn't take most of what they said to heart, but Tythus didn't like them. They had nothing in common with one another. Khlaux was too honorable. Elizer too whimsical.

He drew one of his new knives, looked at it, and started picking at his teeth. The point poked his gum, drawing blood. "Damn." He needed to be more careful.

At dinner, Surtz served them a delicious meal. When his brothers finished and excused themselves, Tythus remained seated. He thought about what tomorrow might bring. About how he was going to leave this city, and hopefully never return. Tythus wondered where he'd end up. Where he'd go. Who he'd meet. He wondered if he'd ever see his family again, then realized it didn't matter. Tythus wanted his own life. A life away from his grandmother.

"Tskah."

Tythus looked up and found Surtz standing nearby, watching him.

"My lord, is something wrong?"

"No, Surtz. Do you enjoy working here?"

"The Corbéo family has always been a prideful and wonderful—"

"Surtz. Speak freely."

"I fucking hate it, sir."

"Tomorrow morning, make sure you sweep under my bed."

"Sir?"

"That is all, Surtz. I need some rest."

Surtz, confused, nodded, and continued cleaning.

Tythus went to his room, double-checked everything was in order, and then counted his coin. He sorted out enough to pay Ailose the promised amount, and a significant portion for his own financial needs. Then he put the rest of the coin into a pouch, sliding it under his bed. For Surtz. The man could go free. *Nobody deserves to be stuck with my grandmother.* And Surtz was a good man.

Confident in his plans, Tythus went to sleep earlier than normal, eager to meet with Ailose and intending to avoid his brothers, or Surtz.

He woke at dawn. Using the slim amount of light peeking through his window, he gathered his possessions and snuck out. When he closed the front door behind him, he breathed a sigh of relief. This was it. He was leaving. Smiling, Tythus hurried away from the Corbéo residence.

When he arrived at the alleyway across from Elph's

leatherworking, Tythus found Ailose, pack strapped on his shoulders, a long brown traveler's cloak, and a sword at his hip.

"Aye, ready to leave Lochwall, T?"

"You bet." Tythus removed his pack, retrieving a sack of coin. "Your second payment."

Something smacked into the cobblestones behind Tythus. He turned and saw a figure standing nearby, cloaked in black robes. The figure who'd been following him, he was certain of it. Instincts kicked in and Tythus drew his knife.

"Drop it," the figure said.

Tythus hunched, making himself smaller. "Make me." He heard Ailose's sword being drawn.

The figure shrugged, then raised a finger and made a gesture. His other hand produced a cudgel from beneath his cloak.

The whoosh of several crossbows being fired, followed by a grunt, then the clatter of a bolt skidding across the cobblestones.

Tythus turned, then something heavy collided with his head. His vision went black, and he collapsed. Another smack, and he lost consciousness.

Tythus awoke to burning and unbearably bright light. His head pulsed, and his cheek peeled away from stone when he lifted his head. Dried blood caked his face and hair. He gently touched the tender spot where he assumed a cudgel had hit him. Groaning, he sat up, noticed his bag was missing, along with his coin. Several of his knives, gone.

Tythus stood, reeling as the world flipped upside down. He closed his eyes, took a few deep breaths, then opened his eyes. Everything righted itself.

In front of him, Ailose lay face down, several crossbow

bolts sticking out of his back. Tythus didn't have to be a Healer to know the mercenary was dead. Ailose had also been ransacked—his bag was missing.

"Ugh." The plan had been ruined and Tythus wasn't sure what to do. Ailose dead. His grandmother would return home. He couldn't go back. Not like this. She'd know he'd been out in the city. And he'd given enough money for Surtz to leave. How would he explain that?

"Fuck." And now what to do with Ailose? The mercenary had been, for lack of a better term, a friend. He couldn't leave the man sprawled out here. "Where would I put you, though?" It's not like he could bury him. Lochwall was a city and he couldn't drag a body through the populated section. The city guard would arrest him. They'd hang him for murder.

"Fuck. Fuck. *Fuck.*" He panicked. "What do I do?" He could leave the body, but he didn't want to do that to Ailose.

Then a stench wafted by. He wrinkled his nose. It smelled like shit. He realized it must've been the sewers. Tythus knew about tunnels that swept under the city, carrying the resident's waste beyond the walls. He'd heard there were access points in the poorer sections of towns. Sometimes, a clog needed to be removed. Whichever unfortunate urchin fixed it often developed disease, and died, but not before receiving a significant sum of money.

Ailose's body lay there, decaying in the sun. He couldn't leave the man here for long. *But dump him in the sewer?* It was the best he could offer the man. The closest thing to a burial, and the best way Tythus could avoid being caught. As long as he could discard the body without being seen.

Tythus left the body behind, exited the alleyway, and entered the next alley over. About halfway down, he spotted a sewer grate. There was a lock on it, and he had no key. No way to open it. No way to break it. He wished he knew how to pick locks. Dejected, he didn't know what to do.

A voice croaked from behind him. "Want it open?"

Tythus turned and saw a dirty, frail woman.

"Want it open?" she asked again.

"Can you?"

"I could." She coughed, shaky hand reaching up to cover her mouth. Red spots dotted her skin. Something was wrong with her.

"Please."

She waved him away, produced a small metal piece, and picked the lock. After a few moments, she opened the grate.

"There you go," she rasped.

"Thank you." If he'd had his money, he would've given her enough for a month of food. "I don't... I don't have anything."

"We look after our own." She turned around and hobbled away.

One of our own? Just how bad did he look?

He forgot the words of the vagabond and returned to Ailose. Tythus, using all his strength, worked on dragging the heavy man towards the sewer. When he got to the end of the alleyway, his energy dissipated, and he fell to his knees, exhausted.

The raspy woman returned. "A friend of yours?" Several hideous-looking people followed her.

"He was murdered."

"We saw," one of the newcomers said.

"What?" Tythus asked. "You watched them attack us?"

A different one answered. "Yes. We don't intervene with questionable city guard or guild affairs. If we did, they'd kill us, too."

That's probably true.

The raspy woman turned and whispered to the others. They walked over to Ailose and lifted him. "We take care of our own," she said.

Tythus stumbled after them as the procession carried

Ailose to the sewer entrance. They set the body down, feet placed into the grate, dangling.

"Sorry we can't do more," the woman said and they disappeared, leaving Tythus with Ailose.

He knelt beside the mercenary. "I apologize, Ailose. Wasn't supposed to go this way." Then he gave a shove, and Ailose fell, splashing into the muck. Closing the sewer grate, Tythus looked around, but the others didn't reappear.

He slipped out the alley, through the slums, and exited Lochwall. It was time he grew up, despite not having money. He didn't want to end up like the alleyway-folk.

One year later, and Tythus had made his way from Lochwall to Anepolis. In Anepolis, the capital of Calrym, he'd found nothing permanent. Throughout his year at Anepolis, he found some odd work here and there; enough to scrap together enough money to eat. But there were so many adult men taking the same jobs he was looking for, and nobody wanted to hire a boy over a man.

He went from one job to another, and everyone called him "boy" and told him to get lost or gave him a task to do for a few coins. Tythus used those coins at the cheapest inn he could find, a shady place called A Night's Whisper. There were way louder noises than whispers happening throughout the night, though.

Tythus couldn't afford to rent a room, but the innkeeper allowed Tythus to sleep on a wooden pallet next to the fireplace for cheap. When Tythus wasn't working or pursuing more work, he relaxed in the common room of the inn, listening to patrons talk and watching people perform.

One of these times he spent relaxing, a burly man with sagging jowls and a fat midriff walked into the inn. He wasted no time, didn't purchase a drink, didn't glance at the scanty whores, just peered around at the patrons. "I need workers able to sail and be gone for an extended period. I'll expect you to help load and unload ships, and later in our journey, we will travel to Qothe. It's going to be a long venture, but there'll also be lots of money available. A fair warning though: if you decide halfway through the trip that it's not for you, I'm not willing to let you go. I need the hands. If anyone's interested, and you're not afraid of being gone a year or more, meet us at the western gate tomorrow morning." Then he turned his back on them and retreated outside.

The patrons went back to their drinking and carousing and laughing around. Several remarked the man had been a fool to show up here. Tythus tuned them out, though. He already knew he'd be there in the morning.

That night, before he went to sleep, he settled any outstanding debts he had with the innkeeper and thanked him for his hospitality. Tythus slept one last time on the wooden pallet and woke early the next morning with a stiff back, but a pleasant attitude. He ate a healthy portion of porridge the innkeeper's wife made every morning, before leaving A Night's Whisper and heading to the western gate.

When Tythus arrived, he spotted several pack mules and men, along with Saggy Jowls, packing, unpacking, and repacking supplies.

As Tythus approached the group, Saggy Jowls noticed him. "You come for work, boy?"

He almost answered, then frowned. If he was going to work for these people for an extended period, he'd need their respect. He thought of Lieutenant Caius Bonovak, the Remerian military commander. If Tythus wanted to be strong, he needed a powerful name that wasn't already his. "It's Caius," he said.

"Caius, eh?" Saggy Jowls grinned, holding a fat hand out for Caius to shake. "Nivian Murphos, merchant, trader, and bosun of *Bloodcurdle*—don't let the name intimidate you. The ship's original owner was a pirate who eventually sold it to our benefactor, Chauvice. Chauvice is a rich man who finds good deals and people willing to take on risks, then reaps the rewards. Basically, Chauvice hires us to trade, and he keeps half the profit. Lucky bastard, Chauvice. Anyway, welcome to the crew, Caius."

The crew waited another half hour before Caius left the city with them and their new crewmen. Over the course of the next week, they traveled on foot to Bryn, and when they got to the port town, Caius was shown to the crew's quarters on *Bloodcurdle.* The newly hired crew members selected free hammocks, and then Nivian Murphos directed them as they loaded up the vessel.

The strenuous worked slowed Caius, but he didn't stop. He knew he needed to prove himself. He pushed himself to keep pace with the other workers.

As Caius disembarked to pick up his next load, he spied a man huffing and leaning against a stack of crates, wiping sweat from his forehead.

"I'm not paying you to lounge, Demoux, get back to work!" Nivian Murphy, who was leaning over the bulwark, had done zero work, opting to watch them instead.

It hadn't surprised Caius. The saggy jowls had been one clue. The second was Nivian's rank.

Demoux sighed, glancing up at Nivian. "We can't work all day like this."

"Everyone else does. You're getting beaten by a young man—a near child. Pathetic," Nivian said. Catching the eyes of Caius, he nodded. "Good job, Caius. You keep this up and you'll be well rewarded."

Being well rewarded ended up meaning Caius got a double portion of the slop they were serving for dinner that night. It wasn't all that bad though, because after they ate, Nivian surprised them all with some nochi—a spiced, choco-late ale. And nobody cared if Caius indulged.

Bloodcurdle rested in port a few more days before its captain arrived—a lanky man who reeked of alcohol and body odor. With the captain's return, the ship set sail, and Caius found himself tasked with various duties the other sailors pushed on to him. The work was laborious, and sometimes gross, but Caius filled his body out quickly doing it.

They traveled along the coast of Calrym to Maceport in Remeria, where they traded goods and unloaded, then loaded the ship again. They journeyed to Cyrok and repeated the process. Each time the ship docked in port, they stayed far longer than Caius expected. But, according to Nivian, when Caius had inquired about this, they weren't beholden to any rules. Their benefactor, Chauvice, had little knowledge about such things, or care to know. As long as they returned every so often and dumped money into his hands, Chauvice allowed them to do what they wanted.

A year passed on *Bloodcurdle*, and Caius transitioned from boy to man. The habit he'd developed at picking his teeth with a knife remained, and many a person gave him odd looks.

When he learned they'd be docking at Yordiv in Qothe, he'd secretly decided he wouldn't return to the ship. He'd venture out and see what there was to see.

"Nivian," he said, when *Bloodcurdle* had docked and been unloaded.

"Caius." Nivian handed him a pouch of coin. "Your payment for this delivery."

Caius pocketed the meager amount of money. "I have something else…" he trailed off, unsure of what to say.

Nivian nodded, a sad expression coming to his eyes. "I know that look, son. You aren't the first person to deliver this type of news. You won't be returning to the ship." He laughed, and his jowls shook and flapped. "No matter. You're young enough to explore the world and not be ruined by it. Go, then. Go out and find a purpose. And if you ever end up wanting to return, as long as I'm the bosun of this ship, you'll have a place."

They shook hands and Caius disembarked without saying goodbye to anyone else.

Here's a land that's prosperous, he thought, then snorted. The rocky expanse was nothing compared to the grassy plains, forests, and mountains in Calrym.

Qothe wasn't as hospitable as anywhere he'd ever been. His time spent in Yordiv resulted in several unavoidable bodies of people who'd attempted to rob or kidnap him. After defending himself, Caius found he was adept at killing, and once he'd discovered that, he'd found a few jobs that funded his time in the city, paid for by a group of secretive Magicai. After a while, he'd begun to build a reputation for himself, which he disliked, so he stopped looking for those jobs.

Escaping Calrym had been his primary concern as a boy. He didn't want his grandmother to locate him. He'd heard rumors there was a place called the University of Arcanical Arts, where he could earn a good bit of money for little work, and figured he'd see if he could get some non-violent work there. He spent the night in a friendly, but sweltering, tavern, and was able to secure directions to Ashmount. He left that morning.

Caius wiped sweat from his forehead. There was no shade, no reprieve from the heat. The open landscape held little other than boulders and small weeds and bushes. His shirt stuck to his back, to his neck. His feet were sweating. Caius had to take several breaks to catch his breath, and that was all within the first few hours of walking.

And then, something strange occurred. He saw a dark shape at the base of a mountain. Caius drew a knife, and, nervous, he started poking around his teeth.

A body lay sprawled upon the rocks. Its mouth opened, eliciting a moan. Spooked, he jerked his hand, cutting his gums. Blood dripped out his mouth, down his chin. He swallowed.

"Careful," Caius said. The boy didn't look so good. His legs broken; his face burned. He looked like he'd been drying out in the sun. "Wouldn't want you to hurt yourself." *What the fuck is one supposed to say to a dying man?*

"T-T-Too late," the boy said.

Caius frowned at the stammer. "Hit your head?" Wondered what was wrong with him. Perhaps his injuries.

"B-B-Born with the stutter."

"Born with the burned face and broken legs, too?" He flicked the knife, the point digging into his gum again, missing his teeth. "Looks like you could use some help."

The boy sneered. "Looks like you want an infection in your m-mouth. What are you d-d-doing here?"

"Heard there was an invitation to get tested at the university. For the Trace. Figured I'd see what it was all about. Wouldn't be too bad to be a Magicus." He looked at his knife. *Now what?* He needed to break the habit because the boy was right. The older Caius became, the more habitual the bloody gums had become. He needed to break the cycle.

"D-D-Don't bother. They'll just k-k-kill you," the boy said.

Caius grunted. *All men in power end up murdering excessively.* He noticed a split fingernail. Turned the knife to file it down. "What happened to you?"

"I j-j-jumped off the volcano."

Caius laughed. "What *actually* happened."

The boy just stared at him.

"Oh. You're serious."

"Yes."

He looked at the jagged angles of the boy's legs. "Broke your legs."

"You're a student of observation."

Caius bit back a retort. He had a good feeling about the boy. "You need help."

"Yes."

Well, I'm not going to continue up there just to die. "I'm not doing anything. Suppose I can help you. For a price."

"What d-d-do you want?"

He didn't know. "Interesting question, that. I'll let you know sometime. Until then, I'm Caius."

"D-Demri."

"Let's sit you up."

Caius helped Demri, and, unknown to Caius, he'd spend the rest of his life in Demri's presence. He didn't realize how detrimental that would become.

THE COST OF BUSINESS

Quills, inkpot, a sheaf of documents, legal papers and folders, a small pouch of coins—newly minted at the local bank and sporting a brilliant shine, of course—and his official Roachford and Singleton legal stamp went into the fine leather satchel propped open on the finished mahogany table where he took his meals. It was, frankly, far too nice a table for eating off. Money, however, bought plenty of unnecessary things, and when you had more of it than you knew what to do with, you spent it frivolously, needlessly, on items of extravagance. Or, perhaps, you didn't. But those people, he figured, weren't living life to its fullest.

He closed the flap of the satchel, snapping the button and revealing the embossed Roachford and Singleton's silver insignia engraved on the outside of the bag. Then he retrieved his black long coat, ensured every crease was correct, every button snapped and shined to its brightest, and slipped a kerchief in his front pocket—one never knew when a kerchief would come in handy. He felt the rise of acid in his stomach and let out a silent burp. In another pocket he had a tin of ground ginger, which he took a pinch from, stuffing it into his mouth. Sometimes the ginger helped prevent the regurgitation and burning.

Flinging the satchel over his shoulder, the familiar weight of the bag around felt almost welcome. Like an old friend. He'd been in this business for several decades now, he and his partner both, and some things didn't change. *Fletchward.* He remembered his task for the day—Arcandus Fletchward—and stifled a groan.

The necessities packed away, his immaculate appearance completed, Stetzler Roachford exited his manor, nodding to that day's doorman/guard. He didn't know the man's name, didn't want to know it. Keep things professional and people will remain alert. Too often he'd seen it—somebody befriend somebody else, and, because of said friendship, they relaxed. They got lazy, let things slip. They stopped being afraid.

His partner, Govitch Singleton, large, hulking, and meaty, stood waiting for him. A small pair of glasses perched low on his nose. Despite having all the wealth in the world, Govitch never bothered getting them tightened. His finger raised, pressing the glasses back up his nose. "Fletchward still?" Govitch asked.

"Yes," Stetzler said. Even now he could identify his own voice as nasally—something that'd bothered him as a young child. Other children had pointed it out in their ruthless, mocking way. It had stuck with him until adulthood. Until the formation of Roachford and Singleton's. For the past two plus decades, with Govitch Singleton's partnership, they'd formed a burgeoning business with the establishment of their law offices. He'd become both rich and powerful; the sound of his voice didn't matter anymore. "I'd like to check in with Percius first."

Govitch nodded, pushing the glasses back up his nose. Despite having enough money to hire armed help, Govitch refused to rid himself of the ugly mace hanging from his belt. He'd grown up a brawler, he'd once said, and would remain one until his death. Stetzler had argued against this as it was an enormous breach of professionalism in law. Once Govitch had prevented Stetzler's death twice, he'd conceded. Govitch could have the mace. Stetzler had been adamant about wearing a proper suit, though—something Govitch wasn't fond of.

Together, Stetzler and Govitch followed a pair of hired guards down several cobblestone streets in Anepolis, Calrym, the capital of the world. Once they'd made a name for themselves, they'd both agreed their headquarters would be in the wealthiest and most prestigious city of the wealthiest and most powerful country. Their hired guardsmen were large enough and held a reputation as employees of Roachford and Singleton's, their mere presence was enough to frighten most people out of their paths.

In the heart of Anepolis, on the busiest street corner, the headquarters of Roachford and Singleton's towered over most of the other businesses. The law office, with instructions detailed by Stetzler himself, was a massive stone building, complete with a pair of thick pillars flanking its entrance, beautifully carved arched windows filled with stained glass, and sloped roofing. Stenciled in large gold lettering above the doorway: Roachford and Singleton's Law Headquarters. Acquiring the space to construct the building had been an enormous cost—they'd had to buy out four other businesses, knock down their buildings, and then fit theirs in the smaller-than-realized space that was left behind. Somehow, the workers had done it. And now, Roachford and Singleton's was the most expensive business in Anepolis.

Before proceeding to the door, Stetzler turned to the guardsmen. "Wait for us here. We'll be requiring your escort later, as we'll need to visit Arcandus Fletchward in person."

The guardsmen nodded and Stetzler and Govitch approached the Roachford and Singleton's headquarters.

"Master Roachford, Master Singleton," the doorman said, offering a slight bow. He pulled open the door, revealing the marble tiled interior. "Welcome."

Stetzler ignored the doorman, but Govitch, though he talked little elsewhere, offered his customary response. "Greetings on this fine and wunnerful day." Stetzler had long ago forgiven his partner's decision to pronounce that word incorrectly.

Boots clicked and echoed on the shined marble floors, and a thud rang through the chamber as the doorman shut the door behind them.

"Ahh," a voice to Stetzler's left said. "Master Roachford, Master Singleton. How fortunate you've arrived." A scrawny man, with eyes too large for his face and a nose too small, rose from his great, high-backed chair—which looked more throne than seat—and scurried around the obtrusive desk he required to "maintain an organized demeanor". Percius Harbridge, the headquarters manager, clutched a file to his chest. "I presume you're looking for this information, Master Roachford?" He closed his eyes, dipping his head in that self-satisfied way he had, and proffered the sheaf of papers to Stetzler.

Stetzler took the folder. He noticed Arcandus Fletchward's name scrawled on its front. *Perfect.* Percius always provided Stetzler what he needed before he asked. It was why Stetzler allowed Percius his throne-like chair and too-large desk.

"Very good, Percius."

Percius smiled for but a moment before he dove into his daily report. "I've left each of you a tentative schedule on your desks for the next several days. Master Singleton, don't forget you're to meet with Ms. Belvadore this evening. She's distraught over the loss of her champion spaniels. Master Roachford, a missive was dropped off regarding the damage to Garland Chaustis's manor. I believe he's discovered the men contracted to repair the original damage weren't, in fact, experienced in construction. He claims they have fled the city, but despite my best assurances that we don't run a bounty hunter service here, he was quite adamant we track down the city guard and set them on the trail of these miscreants. I promptly informed him he needed to—"

"Enough," Stetzler said, cutting Percius off.

"Will either of you require anything else then, sirs?" Percius asked.

"No," Stetzler said, waving the folder. "We came for this."

Percius smiled. "Of course, Master Roachford. If you wish an update or would like to hear the extended list of topics we haven't yet discussed—but which require your *immediate* attention—I'll be right here." He scurried back round his desk, planting his slender frame in the center of his throne. Dipping a quill tip into an inkwell, he went back to work.

Stetzler rifled through the papers, ensuring the information he needed was there. Arcandus Fletchward had hired Roachford and Singleton's, suing his former employer, alleging malpractice and wrongful termination. Fletchward's former employer was the Anepolis city guard. Any normal guardsman wouldn't be able to afford, nor had the connections or proof to pursue litigation against the Calrym government. Arcandus Fletchward, however, was not a normal guardsman. He'd worked as the official chancellery of the guard for the capital city, recording and filing every prisoner's status, every reported crime, every ongoing case.

Fletchward had alleged he was made to practice nefarious deeds in order to speed casework along or incriminate a particular prisoner. Stetzler cared for none of that. Under normal circumstances, Roachford and Singleton's wouldn't have taken such a case. However, a case against the government meant a very large and guaranteed payday—the funds would come out of the already established city treasury—as long as they won the case. The problem, however, was that Arcandus Fletchward wasn't cooperating, nor had he paid the retainer Roachford and Singleton's required. This case, though, was not one Stetzler planned on letting lapse, despite a lack of payment. Too much money involved to neglect the case.

Arcandus Fletchward's file contained pertinent information Stetzler and Govitch would need: his personal finances and banking information, receipts of spendings at local businesses—investments and purchases Fletchward had made that he wouldn't know Stetzler and Govitch could procure from people who owed them favors, and a variety of other information Stetzler and Govitch already had, such as each of Fletchward's allegations against the city guard and examples of their criminal behavior, all rounded up neatly by Percius.

"Govitch," he said. "We have what we need." Stetzler slipped the file into his satchel. "Would you believe Arcandus Fletchward bought stock in multiple businesses last week?"

Govitch gasped, pausing a moment to push his glasses back up his nose. "Incredulous."

"And according to the bank, he has multiple accounts, all recently depleted."

"Abhorrent."

"It would appear, Govitch, our client has also sold a property for double its value."

"Insufferable."

"One wonders where said money disappeared to, because all his accounts are empty."

"Incomprehensible."

"It is, unfortunately, a prospect of modern times," Stetzler said, shaking his head. There were many clients they'd rejected for similar reasons. Roachford and Singleton's got their due, or they didn't take the case. Fletchward was only lucky he was suing the government.

"I'm assuming we're not doing this for free," Govitch said,

smiling. It was a regular routine they had. Pretending they didn't already know what they were doing. It made work fun. And work was supposed to be fun, right?

"Of course not, Govitch. One must collect their debts."

Govitch nodded, his glasses sliding down the bridge of his nose. He pushed them back up. "One must not ignore the cost of business."

"I feel most sorry for Arcandus Fletchward," Percius said from behind his desk. He was sitting straight up in the throne-chair, watching them with his bulging eyes. "But if you keep up this charade, I'm afraid you'll end up missing the trial."

Stetzler, had he been a younger version of himself, might've rolled his eyes at the comment. Instead, he just stared at Percius. "Are you so free of work you're able to bicker with your employers?"

"No, sir," Percius said, his face diving towards the desk, quill already in hand, the scratching of his writing on parchment music to Stetzler's ears. Percius peeked up at Stetzler for a moment before saying, "I wish you well with Arcandus, Master Roachford, Master Singleton."

"Very good, Percius," Stetzler said. "I enjoy an employee who can keep himself occupied."

Percius didn't answer, which satisfied Stetzler.

"Percius," Stetzler said, already knowing the answer but asking anyway to show his authority, "where might one locate Mr. Fletchward at this hour?"

Percius looked back up from his document, offering a wide, disingenuous smile. "Master Roachford, I'm sure you'd find Arcandus at his home. He lives in a small apartment above the Cheesehouse, but I'm sure you already knew that, sir."

"Of course, Percius, thank you. What would we do without you?"

Percius didn't answer, which satisfied Stetzler again.

"To the Cheesehouse, Govitch."

"Affirmative."

Stetzler and Govitch exited the building. Stetzler ignored the doorman's well wishes, while Govitch returned the sentiment, and then they rejoined their guardsmen.

The Cheesehouse was three streets away from Roachford and Singleton's, off the main market streets, placed on a respectable corner. Their escort weaved their way through civilians, paving the way for Stetzler and Govitch. Once they'd escaped the first two roads, the crowds cleared to a manageable amount, allowing them to walk without issue.

Stetzler's nose wrinkled at the familiar stench of pungent cheese. An expensive apartment Arcandus had not. The storefront had a wide glass window display of a variety of signs, each with depictions and descriptions of fresh cheeses and other dairy products, along with their current stock status. A bell tinkled as a guardsman opened the front door to the Cheesehouse, stepping aside to admit Stetzler and Govitch.

Inside, the ripe odor intensified and Stetzler removed the kerchief in his long coat, placing the cloth over his mouth and nose, eyes narrowing in disgust. *You never know when you'll need a kerchief.*

An employee garbed in a yellow apron and yellow hat and yellow gloves, and, if Stetzler had any say in it, a yellow personality, hurried over to greet them. "Welcome, welcome my friends, to the Cheesehouse," he beamed like the sun—a far too-happy grin on his face—spreading his hands in front of him, as if he owned the place. He didn't, he was just an employee working for a wealthy noblewoman—Stetzler had researched the building to learn more about his client. The silence built between them for a moment, and the employee's thin mustache twitched.

A moment later, then Stetzler said, "Regrettably, we're here on other business matters. I'm Stetzler Roachford, and this is my partner..." He paused, allowing Govitch to introduce himself.

"Govitch Singleton," Govitch said. He used his middle finger to slide his glasses back into place.

"We're here to visit with Arcandus Fletchward."

"Oh," the employee said, face morphing into disappointment. Then his yellow personality returned and the man, beaming like the sun, flashed his yellow teeth at them. "Well, don't let a cheese worker prevent the good work of the law!" He grinned, backing away from them, hands held up as if Stetzler was an officer, not a lawyer.

"Thank you," Stetzler said.

A pair of guardsmen led the way to the stairs in the back of the business, which led to the second floor. The other guardsmen waited outside. They'd completed this routine countless times, knew what Stetzler and Govitch expected.

Stetzler followed the pair of guardsmen, long coat flapping at his heels with each step he ascended, Govitch's thundering footsteps behind him. At the top of the staircase they entered another door, into a cramped hallway with a pair of doors on either side. Two small apartments. Stetzler placed the kerchief back in his pocket, the stench of cheese somewhat abated, and a need for professionalism and an intimidating presence overpowering his desire to shield his face with a cloth.

A guardsman's fist pounded on the left door. "Arcandus Fletchward?"

No answer. The guardsman repeated himself, knocking harder. The door rattled, and Stetzler wondered what Fletchward's neighbor thought of the event—no doubt they could hear everything.

"Roachford and Singleton's, Mr. Fletchward. You can't turn us away," the guardsman said, rapping on the door a third time. He knocked so hard, Stetzler found himself surprised the door remained on its hinges.

They waited a moment. Nothing.

"Sir?" the guardsman asked.

"Break the—"

The door opened. A disheveled Arcandus Fletchward stood in the doorway. "Why are you here so early?"

"It's midday, Mr. Fletchward," Stetzler said.

Govitch nudged Stetzler aside, placing his large hand on Fletchward's shoulder. "Move," he said, giving Fletchward a shove.

Fletchward toppled backward with a yelp, and Govitch, followed by Stetzler, then the two guardsmen, piled into the cramped apartment.

"What are you doing here?" Fletchward asked. He held his head in one hand, though Stetzler knew he hadn't hit it. Judging by the scent of alcohol and vomit, he was nursing a hangover.

"I am your lawyer, Mr. Fletchward," Stetzler said.

Govitch snorted. "We're."

"*We're* your lawyers, Mr. Fletchward."

"And?" Fletchward asked, squinting and wincing through what Stetzler could only assume was a sudden headache.

"You haven't paid your retainer fee, Mr. Fletchward," Stetzler said. He frowned, reaching into a pocket in his long coat and pulling out the tin of ginger. He popped the lid, offering it to Fletchward. "Ginger. It'll help the nausea."

"I'm fine," Fletchward said, waving away the tin.

"Yes, well, I'm afraid that's about to change, Mr. Fletchward." Stetzler covered the tin, dropping it back in its place. "Do you have the retainer fee you owe us?"

"No. I've already told you—I don't have the money."

"Mr. Fletchward," Stetzler said, unsnapping his satchel and retrieving Fletchward's file. "I have reason to believe otherwise." He flipped through the parchments, locating several he was searching for. "All of this evidence is recent. And by 'recent' I mean since you first hired Govitch and me.

First," he dropped the parchment, letting it fall to the floor by Fletchward, who'd still not stood back up. "You made two stock purchases in businesses. The bank and, for some ill-conceived idea, the building you live in—the Cheesehouse." Stetzler found himself wrinkling his nose at the mere thought of the cheese stench, though he couldn't notice it over the aroma of alcohol and vomit.

"Stetzler, Govitch, I apologize, truly, but—"

Stetzler dropped another piece of parchment. "You held several extravagant parties at various inns, hosting dozens of people and paying the tab for all of them."

"I know, I know, but I'll—"

Stetzler let the third piece of parchment fall, the second to last he'd picked from the file. "You purchased three prized horses as a surprise present for Duke Harlem Maccaro and his daughter."

"Yes, I know that, but I promise—" Fletchward stopped, holding his head with both hands for a moment. Stetzler let him fight through the headache. "I promise I'll pay you."

Stetzler let the last piece of parchment go. "That's a record of your current accounts—yes, from all your banks—and you don't have the money, Arcandus." He stopped with the polite routine. It was time for the hard truth. "You don't have the money, and you will not have the money. You're broke. Broke and without a means to collect the money you already owe to half the businesses in Anepolis. What you're doing spending all of this money like you're a duke yourself is pathetic and low. If you were a normal client of Govitch and me, we'd drop you. But, Arcandus Fletchward, you are not. You have a legitimate case against the government. And so, we have taken on your case regardless."

"Thank you, Stetzler, Govitch. I am in your debt." Fletchward bowed his head to the ground, his forehead touching the floor. Stetzler couldn't tell if the action was taken in deference or because of hangover pains.

"I insist you take some of this," Stetzler said, retrieving the tin of ginger. He popped the top and offered it.

"Thank you," he said. Fletchward took a pinch of the ginger, shoving it into his mouth.

"Good, good," Stetzler said. He covered the tin once again, placing it in his pocket. Now for the hard part. He grabbed his kerchief from the other pocket. "Here."

Fletchward looked up, swallowing the ginger, and saw the kerchief in confusion.

"One never knows when a kerchief will come in handy," Stetzler said. "Take it."

"For what?"

"Cleaning," Govitch said, stepping forward.

The two guardsmen they'd brought with them straightened, striking an imposing and dominating barricade in front of the only door that led out of Fletchward's apartment.

"Cleaning what?" Fletchward stood, frowning at the guardsmen, glancing at Govitch, then at Stetzler. "What are you doing?"

"We don't work for free, Mr. Fletchward," Stetzler said, returning to his professionalism. "We must make sure you understand the ramifications of not paying us our due."

"I understand, Stetzler. I'll have the money—"

"You haven't been listening, Arcandus." Some people just didn't pay attention. Those were the people who irritated Stetzler the most. He grit his teeth for but a moment, taking a deep breath through his nose and exhaling via his mouth. "Sit." Stetzler pointed at the small wooden table Fletchward clearly took his meals at.

Confused, Fletchward rose from the floor and took a spot at the table. Stetzler and Govitch followed him.

"Place your hand on the table," Stetzler said. Fletchward, still appearing confused, obeyed. Stetzler flung the kerchief next to Fletchward's hand. "Put that to the side. Govitch?"

Govitch drew a large knife from his belt, placing it on the table. "Knife," he said, helpfully.

"You have two options, Arcandus," Stetzler said, holding two fingers up like he was teaching a child. "The first is, you take that knife, you select a finger on that hand, and cut it off."

He blanched, staring up at Stetzler, skin turning pale. "What?"

"You heard me."

"I can get money, Stetzler. This is going a bit far, don't you think? I mean, who in their right mind would hire somebody that threatens to cut the fingers off their clientele? Once news of this gets out, nobody would come to you." Fletchward laughed.

"People who want to hire the best. People who understand that we are a no-nonsense business. We asked you when you first came to us if you could afford our fee. You said yes. If you had not said this, we could have discussed options because this case, your case, has a very strong possibility of paying out a handsome settlement. You assured us, Arcandus. You told us we'd have our money. We've confronted you no less than *three* times. Still, we have seen no money. The paperwork has been filed. The courts are ready. Your case is going to be heard. You need us, now. Without us, you'll not win. And if you lose, you won't have another opportunity to sue the government—they'll make sure of that. So, either you walk into a secret hideaway and find that money, or you can pick one of our two fine alternative options."

"Give me a week. I'll have your money."

"Roachford and Singleton's doesn't wait. We've given you plenty of time."

"Lots," Govitch said. He crossed his thick arms, puffed his chest out, stared down at Fletchward like he was a bug. Which, compared to Govitch, he was.

"What is the alternative, then?" Fletchward asked.

"We already told you one of them." Stetzler gestured at the knife. "The second one is that instead of cutting your own finger off, you'll sign over everything you own to us."

"What?" Fletchward's jaw dropped and a flush of red creeped across his cheeks.

Govitch pushed his glasses up his nose, patting the mace hanging at his belt. "It's the cost of business," Govitch said.

"Can you imagine if we let every fool like yourself off easy?" Stetzler asked. "Every time somebody gambled away their money? Every time somebody spent it foolishly on a business investment—say, investing in a fucking dairy store? Our reputation would mirror that of yours, Arcandus—zero respect." Stetzler took a moment and cleared his throat. In a softer, kinder tone, he said, "We'd prefer you select option one. It's less work for all involved and we don't have to deal with this..." he waved his hand around the room, "...mess you call a 'business'. We just want the money that's owed."

"There's got to be a better way. A better way for all of us," Fletchward said.

"There was. But you missed that deadline, Arcandus."

"Knife," Govitch said, reaching out and sliding it an inch closer to Fletchward.

"I can't believe—"

"Believe it, Arcandus. And know this: completing either option doesn't absolve you of your debt. It does, however, grant you the extension you're so desperate for. We'll take what you owe from the awarded money, assuming we win this case—which should be an easy victory, plus interest."

Fletchward swallowed, nodding. He bowed his head, reached out and grasped the knife with his right hand. The knife rattled, shaking in his grip. He looked back up at Fletchward, quivering, a tear dripping from his left eye.

"Make it quick, so you don't have to saw through the bone," Govitch said.

Fletchward let out a squeak of panic and swallowed again. "I, please. I can't do this."

Stetzler nodded, using his understanding tone to answer. "There is always option two, Arcandus."

"What? N-n-no. Option one." He spread the fingers on his left hand out on the wooden table, angling the blade's point at the base of his pinky finger. He swallowed again, knife tapping against the table as Fletchward trembled.

"Chop," Govitch said.

Fletchward closed his eyes, took a deep breath, and brought the knife down. He screamed in pain, and blood squirted across the wooden table, while a loud crack indicated the severing of bone. Fletchward lifted his hand. The pinky fell from its rightful place, dangling by a string of sinew. Blood streamed down his wrist and his hand started shaking. Fletchward let out a horrified yell.

Govitch reached out, took hold of the pinky, and gave a quick yank. The sinew broke, and Fletchward screamed again. "Pleasure doing business," he said. Govitch tossed the pinky on the table. "Here's your change."

"Don't be late next time, Arcandus," Stetzler said. "Cover the wound with kerchief. Apply pressure. And I do hope you're not out of alcohol." He turned, and with Govitch at his heel, they left Fletchward to his pain.

Sometimes, the cost of business was more than some could afford. When that happened, Stetzler and Govitch made sure they weren't the ones who lost out.

A week later, they took the case to trial. Arcandus Fletchward never mentioned how he lost his pinky, though rumor ran rampant. For a while, Roachford and Singleton's had to deal with client hesitation because of these rumors. Money, however, is often something that cannot wait, and these hesitations often disappeared when somebody's need grew strong enough. Another week after the trial began, Roachford and Singleton's won their case, as predicted. They took thirty-five percent of the money awarded to Arcandus Fletchward, and a month later, claimed the rest after a former coworker of Fletchward's murdered him for implicating him in his crimes. It wasn't ever clear to the public if Roachford and Singleton's were behind it—something Stetzler didn't care.

Everything would work out, if you had a mind for it. But not everyone is aware of the cost of business.

THE BATTLE OF LEEWARD

Captain Edelbrock Brendis spat some skachi juice. He watched it drool from his mouth, sway in the wind, before plummiting to the ground. He noticed it left a smear on his horse's side. Edelbrock hadn't leaned far enough out or, perhaps, the wind had blown it back. Grimacing, he shifted the roll of leaves in his mouth. A pungent taste of moldy damp leaves was all he thought of the addictive substance his soldiers swore on. *I won't be trying this shit again.* But it was already in his mouth and he would not give his soldiers the satisfaction of watching him discharge the drug.

He remained on the plains, mounted on his horse, watching the meadow, soldiers behind him. Watching, waiting. The Vessian Incursion, as the war had been named, was now in its fourth year. The Camel Clans—nomadic warriors from varying clans—had attacked both Calrym and Remeria.

Next to him, Major Vosheim steadied his white steed. "Calm down, nothing's happening," the major said. But that didn't stop either the major or Edelbrock from staring into the distance, watching, waiting.

Major Vosheim commanded a force of eight hundred—a

small amount, when compared to the rest of the Calrite military. Most of the Calrym army was here, camped on the leeward side of the Valkyrnd Mountains. Dust and sand swirled, impending visibility, and yet, still, they stared. Watching, waiting.

"Doesn't appear as if'n they're gonna attack today, eh, Major?" Sergeant Ambers, a thick man with a thicker accent, said. Unlike Edelbrock and Vosheim, Sergeant Ambers paced the lines on the ground. They only had so many horses, and those went to either men of high ranking or the cavalry.

"Unlikely, Sergeant," Vosheim said. He cradled his helm in his arm, wet, sweaty hair hanging in twisted strands just brushing his shoulders. A scar crossed down his eye, and passed through his nose, which was missing a chunk. Vosheim had once joked about this, saying, "Better I lost part of the sniffer, rather than the looker. I got too many things to see, and not one of them I could give a shit about if it stinks." Vosheim cleared his throat, then made a wild motion of shaking his head. Wet hair smacked against his face and, if Edelbrock was a betting man, he would've guessed if there'd been women about they all would've crooned and swayed and begged the man to lie with them.

He thought back to home, where his lover was. *Beautiful woman.* Jaylena Maccaro. Duke's daughter. How he'd convince her father to marry him was something he had yet to figure out. They'd pledged themselves to each other, though, and now he needed something, anything, to offer her father. A promise of fortune. A solid career. Something. But a mere captain in the army wasn't likely to impress a Duke of the kingdom who regularly interacted with the King of Calrym.

"All right, Sergeant, stand the men down. Get ready for a hot meal," Major Vosheim said.

"Yes, sir."

"Captain Brendis," Major Vosheim said, twisting in his

saddle to look at him. "It appears the Camel Clans have taken today off. Ride over to Major Sahl's, see if there's been any orders from the top." He rolled his eyes. "As if they have any clue what in Mother Avani's name we're doing here. Be quick, Captain. I want you organizing tonight's patrol schedule."

Edelbrock saluted. "Yes, sir." *Bastard.* Making the nightly patrol schedules pissed many people off. There was one good thing about having to travel over to Major Sahl's encampment —he leaned over his stallion and near-vomited the glob out.

"Ha, told you the captain couldn't handle it!"

Edelbrock glanced over and glared at the soldier. "Would *you* like to come face-to-face with Major Sahl while *you* had this shit in your mouth?"

The soldier—something Camron—Edelbrock could never remember the man's first name, blanched. "No," he said a moment later, a sheepish look etched on his stupid face.

"That's what I thought," Edelbrock said. "You get mid-shift for patrol, Camron."

"Damn it," Camron said.

"Excuse me?"

"Damn it, *sir.*"

Edelbrock shook his head, but steered his horse around toward Major Sahl's camp. It only took a few sweltering minutes to cross the distance on horseback to the adjacent encampment.

He rode through groups of soldiers who were winding down. Some stoked cooking fires, while others tended to their horse, still others stood about smoking or chewing skachi, and Edelbrock noticed a pair of men sneaking behind a tent. He swore he saw them share a kiss or two. *I'll report that to Major Sahl.* Fraternization during battle often caused unnecessary drama.

Major Sahl's command tent rested in the center of the camp, as custom dictated. Two guards sat on upturned barrels outside the tent flaps, a folded table between them, playing cards. They glanced up at Edelbrock, and one of them pointed at a hitching post where Major Sahl's stallion was tethered. Edelbrock recognized the beautiful, sleek black beast.

"He's in the tent already, sir," one of them said.

He slid off his mount, wrapping the reins around the post, then passed by the guardsmen, who nodded.

"Major's in a mood today, sir," the other said.

Edelbrock returned the nod in thanks, then entered Major Sahl's tent. The interior was more cramped than Edelbrock would've guessed. On one side was Major Sahl's bed, a closed chest, and a small... *bookshelf?* Rows of books lined the three shelves. Perplexed, he shifted his gaze to the major, who sat behind a desk on the other half of the text. Edelbrock found himself standing on an entrance rug, a two-foot by two-foot square of free space on the floor.

Major Sahl peered up at Edelbrock from behind several stacks of parchment. Edelbrock saw maps, letters, and historical documents spread out on the desk.

"Captain." Major Sahl stood, reaching out a hand to shake Edelbrock's. His thick black mustaches arched upwards, forming a frown, but Edelbrock knew by now Major Sahl had an unconscious penchant for appearing angry at all times.

Edelbrock grasped the major's hand, giving a strong, respectable shake. People like Major Sahl required a show of power or they'd instantly dismiss a man as useless.

"Major Sahl, sir."

"You're Vosheim's man, yes?"

"Yes, sir. Major Vosheim wants to know if you've heard anything from up top."

The major snorted. "If only. They're too busy drinking and arguing about coin. Their last orders remain the same: kill as many camel fuckers as we can." Major Sahl snorted, mustaches twitching as his upper lip curled into a sneer. "I hate the savages. They're dirty, honorless, and, if I could wager money, I'd bet they're cannibals. Always fighting with one another. Why they finally attacked us, I'll never understand. Got to beat them into submission, eh? Perhaps they'll hoist up their balls and attack on the morrow. I'm sick of waiting. We're all tired of this game they're playing, these constant raids. Why don't they fucking attack and stay committed to the attack? Nomads. Psh." Major Sahl spat into the sand and glared past Edelbrock, as if he was staring through the tent and into the horde of Camel Clans. His cheeks reddened, if only slightly. "Soon, Captain, soon. We'll get to go home very soon. I feel it."

"We can only hope, sir." Edelbrock wanted to return home, but only after securing some respect. He needed to prove to Jaylena's father he was worthy of marriage. *Jaylena... oh, how I miss you.* He remembered her—the way she looked at him when they stole away in the middle of the night. The taste and feel of her hand wrapping itself around his waist, around his neck, as her plump, moist lips planted themselves upon his mouth. The feeling of her tongue darting in and out of his mouth. His manhood rising as her thigh brushed against him.

"Captain?"

Edelbrock snapped back to the present. "Sir?"

"Tell Vosheim I'll send word if anything comes in from upper leadership. This is the second time he's inquired. Not sure why he thinks they'll send word to me before him. He's a major too. A major nuisance, that is."

"Major Vosheim says you're more respected, more likely to receive the first command."

"Well, he's not wrong there, Captain."

"Yes, sir."

"Dismissed, Captain."

"Yes, sir." Edelbrock exited the tent, annoyed at how fruitless this visitation had been.

He retrieved his horse and returned to Major Vosheim's camp.

"Captain," somebody said.

Edelbrock searched the various campfires until the speaker caught his eye. Camron. Edelbrock sighed. "Yes, Camron?"

"Skulling wants to know if we can switch patrol shifts tonight. He's got first and I'm mid-shift."

Edelbrock arched a brow as Camron spoke. He hadn't been back for a full minute, hadn't had time to even think about who he was assigning where, and already the men were trading shifts they hadn't yet received. "Camron, I haven't assigned a shift yet, aside from yours. But Skulling can have mid-shift if he wants it." Camron let out an exaggerated sigh of relief. "Alongside you," Edelbrock said, spurning his horse back to a slight trot.

"But sir! Captain!"

Edelbrock ignored him and rode to his tent. Waiting next to it was Sergeant Ambers. The big man was cramped inside one of the standard sized chairs. He struggled to heave his body out of it upon seeing Edelbrock.

"Captain," he said.

"Sergeant Ambers." Edelbrock slid off his horse, tethering him nearby, and approached Ambers. "You must be waiting for the shift assignments?"

"Yes, sir."

"I haven't had time to consider it, and I'm supposed to report back to Major Vosheim. Do me a favor and assign them however you wish. I trust you'll be fair."

"Yes, sir. No problem."

"Camron and Skulling are both on mid-shift, though. Understood?"

"No surprise there."

"Not really, no. Thanks, Sergeant."

Sergeant Ambers nodded. "You're welcome."

Edelbrock, exhausted from the long day, glanced at his tent before marching through the camp to make his report. Major Vosheim wasn't like Major Sahl. Sahl was always easy to find. Vosheim, on the other hand, liked to mingle with random soldiers and was rarely alone.

Edelbrock perused the camp, searching for Vosheim amongst the soldiers. Between the campfire smoke and the skachi smoke, breathing became a laborious task. Several minutes of turning down offers to drink with this group, smoke with that group, and an inquiry about which patrol shifts another group would receive, and Edelbrock spied Major Vosheim.

The major was sitting cross-legged, a lit roll of skachi leaves in one hand, a mug of ale in the other. Edelbrock groaned as he approached Vosheim, the man's inebriation already clear. Skachi wasn't a drug, but if anyone smoked enough of it, it contributed to a foggy mind. And alcohol... Well, alcohol was alcohol and the major had obviously had a lot.

"Major Vosheim," Edelbrock said, leering down at the officer. He realized he hadn't masked his expression. Then he realized he didn't care.

"Captain," Vosheim said, slurring his words. "You don'tsh look sho happy to see me."

"Major Sahl had no reports, sir. He says to stop bothering him with inquiries—if he gets any news, he'll inform you immediately. I've delegated command of the shift rotation to Sergeant Ambers, sir." If the major heard it directly from Edelbrock, he couldn't confront Edelbrock for avoiding his duties. And, frankly put, Edelbrock was too damned tired to care about who took what shift. In the major's drunken state, Edelbrock assumed it'd go one of two ways: either the major would be too drunk to care, or he'd fall into the stereotypical rage many drunken men did.

He was lucky, though. Vosheim just nodded, downing another mug of ale that another drunken sod had refilled. They swayed in their drunkenness, heads clicking against one another.

"Good night, sir," Edelbrock said.

"Good night, Sergeant Ambersh," Vosheim said.

Edelbrock retired for the night. He kicked his boots off, climbed into his meager tent, and slept without eating, for he was too exhausted to care.

***

It had felt like he'd only been asleep for a minute when a shout had jolted him awake.

"Captain!" the voice said again.

Edelbrock sat up. "What?"

Silence. Edelbrock blinked away his sleep, realized the man standing in the tent's entrance was Sergeant Ambers. "Sergeant, what happened?" Normally, urgent news would go immediately to Major Vosheim, but the men had learned if Major Vosheim indulged in his vices he became impossible to wake up in time for an actionable response. Thus, they'd started coming to Edelbrock instead.

Sergeant Ambers snapped out of it. "Dead patrol. Two men."

"Who? How? When?"

"Camron and Skulling, sir. They didn't report in during shift change. Found their bodies, but, uh, sir, their heads were a dozen feet away."

If two men had to die, Edelbrock couldn't have chosen a better pair. "Ambers, what time is it?" Camron and Skulling were supposed to be mid-shift patrolmen, but Edelbrock didn't feel like he'd gotten enough sleep for it to be the end of the mid-shift.

"First shift just ended, sir." Sergeant Ambers at least had the decency to look guilty and shameful. Both Camron and Skullings were supposed to be on the mid-shift.

"Why weren't they on the shift I assigned? They shouldn't have been out there."

Sergeant Ambers grimaced before holding up a large pouch of skachi leaves. "I took a bribe from them, sir."

Edelbrock punched the ground. He rose, snatched the pouch of skachi from the sergeant's hands, and pushed the man back outside. A nearby fire warmed several soldiers who appeared to be returning from patrol duty. Edelbrock tossed the pouch into the flames. He swiveled on his heel, returning his attention to Sergeant Ambers, thrusting his forefinger into the sergeant's chest. "You," he said, thrusting his finger into the man's chest hard, slamming it repeatedly as he spoke, "will go out on patrol and will stay out there, ensuring the safety of our men." After a moment's pause, he added through gritted teeth, "All. Night," slamming his finger twice more into the sergeant's chest.

"Yes, sir," Sergeant Ambers said, eyes glued to the fire where a waft of skachi smoke blanketed the surrounding area.

"And stop smoking that shit. It smells terrible. Get the fuck out of here."

"Yes, sir," the sergeant said. "I'm sorry," he mumbled, before hurrying away.

Rubbing his eyes, Edelbrock returned to bed. He struggled to sleep, thoughts returning to home. Although he was used to sleeping on the ground, his back was stiff this night. His thighs were stiff from riding the horse. And, a few minutes later, Edelbrock stiffened elsewhere as he drifted off to sleep, thinking about fucking his lovely Jaylena.

It felt like only a few minutes later and, once again, Edelbrock was rising from sleep. *Another catastrophe.*

"Sir, wake up! We've caught a deserter!"

Edelbrock wiped the sleep from his eyes once again. "What?"

"Captain Ambers, sir. He was caught trying to flee."

Edelbrock stared at the corporal. *What's his name? Dalton? Conwick? I have not a clue.* "Captain Ambers tried to flee, Corporal?"

"He's outside now, sir. Started crying about how life here is too hard—no man should have to suffer these conditions. Last I heard, he was rambling about how the leadership doesn't care about their own men, sir. Ridiculous, I know."

Yes, ridiculous. Corporal… fuck, I don't recall his damn name. He's right, they're numbers in a war, and we'd likely sacrifice any of them if it guaranteed a victory.

"Having said that, sir," the corporal said, "we all understand this is war. Good men are going to die. But good men die without fleeing."

"Indeed. Take me to the traitor."

"Sir."

The corporal led Edelbrock to the perimeter of their camp, where Sergeant Ambers was kneeling in the grass, hands bound behind his back. A few torches carried by soldiers—swords out and pointed at the sergeant—lit their prisoner's teary face up. When Sergeant Ambers saw who was coming, more tears poured down his face, and he began sobbing.

"Don't kill me, Captain, please," he said through his sobs.

"I don't decide," Edelbrock said. "The law does. And you tried to abandon us." Edelbrock turned to one soldier holding a torch. "Get some rope."

The soldier scratched his cheek, looking at the ground. "Sir," he mumbled, then pointed past Edelbrock with his sword point, "already did…" he trailed off, looking ashamed.

"Good. Initiative earns promotions, soldier." Edelbrock

followed the sword point, and in one of the few trees dotting the landscape, he saw another pair of soldiers testing a noose. "Come along," Edelbrock said, walking over to the large oak tree. Ordinarily, he'd have to get approval from Vosheim to do something like this. But Vosheim was passed out, drunk. Among soldiers, there wasn't a worse crime than trying to flee, other than murdering a fellow soldier.

Sergeant Ambers moaned and whined and cried and pleaded as his captors dragged him across the plains.

Edelbrock stopped at the tree, looked at the surrounding soldiers. "Do it however you wish. *Do not* torture him. Understood?"

"Yes, sir," they all said.

"Good."

As Edelbrock walked away, he heard one of them shout out, "hang 'em by the balls!"

Edelbrock shook his head, and once he was a good distance away, he turned, making sure they didn't torture the man. He figured he'd give them the opportunity to enact their own vengeance. It'd both bond them, make them appreciative of Edelbrock—and by extension, the rest of the army's leadership—and, frankly, Edelbrock didn't feel like dealing with it.

The soldiers yanked the sergeant's pants down. *They can't be...*

And, as he witnessed, they took the rope and tried wrapping it around the sergeant's genitals. Somehow, somebody thought they'd got it to work. Disaster struck. They heaved upon the rope and they lifted Sergeant Ambers. Then a terrifying scream and Sergeant Ambers fell from the rope, crashing to the ground.

The sergeant continued screaming, and Edelbrock ran back to the tree. Unfortunately for Sergeant Ambers, the force of the pulley and the weight of his body worked in opposition and he'd torn his genitalia right off.

"Damn it, put him down!" Edelbrock said.

A soldier thrust his sword into the sergeant's gut.

"Not like that!"

Another soldier stabbed the sergeant in the eye, ending him. Blood seeped into the ground, staining the earth, and as the soldier withdrew his sword, a gray glob of brain oozed out of the sergeant's face.

"All of you!" Edelbrock said. The soldiers snapped to attention, appearing both ashamed and worried. "Resume your patrols. There won't be any disciplinary actions tonight. Just… don't hang somebody by their balls again."

Furious, but also amused—and disgusted—Edelbrock stormed back to his tent. He crawled back into his bedroll and clamped his eyes shut. Fate laughed at him though, because while nobody bothered Edelbrock for the rest of the night, he wasn't able to get more than a few minutes of sleep.

When Edelbrock conceded there wouldn't be more sleep to gain, he crawled out of his bedroll, exiting the tent. Bright sunlight blinded him, even though it had no right to be there. But, in the plains, the sun came early whether or not you liked it.

The corporal who'd woken him in the night appeared as Edelbrock drank his fill of water. Corporal Conton. The name suddenly returned to Edelbrock's memory as he looked at Conton's face.

"Sir," Conton said. "We're to prepare for war."

"Oh?"

"The major says we can't allow what happened to Camron and Skulling to pass. Regardless on if they attack us or not, we're initiating a confrontation."

Edelbrock nodded. They'd been skirmishing on and off with the Camel Clans for far too long. It was time to resolve this.

"Your horse has already been saddled, sir," Conton said.

"Thank you, Corporal."

Edelbrock took a few moments to get his equipment in

order before mounting his horse and navigating through the still-organizing soldiers. He spied Major Vosheim on horseback, relaying orders to various officers. Edelbrock galloped over, ready to receive his orders.

"Ah, Captain, good. I heard you handled nasty business regarding Sergeant Ambers last night. Excellent job." For all the major had indulged the previous night, he showed no symptoms, other than heavy eyelids. That was normal, though. He was good at rising early, regardless of what he'd done hours before.

Probably because he gets a full night's sleep. Edelbrock gave half-a-smile, resisting the urge to reach over and throttle Major Vosheim. "No problem, sir."

"Yes, too bad for Ambers, though. He wasn't a poor soldier."

"No, sir, no, he wasn't."

"Major Sahl has given up waiting for orders. We're to attack today. Our good friend has decided to take point in the battle—I guess he is offended the Clans haven't attacked but have resorted to night raids. Majors Burbaton and Stylos are reinforcing the initial attack. Major Nuremlock and I are to flank when the opportunity presents itself. Understood, Captain?"

"Yes, sir." Edelbrock didn't need to hear the commands to have guessed Major Vosheim's forces would be secondary to the initial attack. Edelbrock had noticed Major Vosheim took a more passive role in the war when possible. He wasn't sure if it was because Major Vosheim felt a duty to his soldiers to keep them alive or if the major feared for his wellbeing. Either way, Edelbrock wouldn't trust Major Vosheim if they ended up back-to-back in battle.

"Relay our orders to Corporal Conton and keep the men vigilant. We don't want to miss our opportunity to aid our fellow soldiers, Captain." Major Vosheim brushed his long hair from his face, spitting a strand from his mouth.

Edelbrock steered his mount around, and he wondered if Major Vosheim cared more about his hair appeared than the battle that could end the war.

He caught the sound of trumpeting horns in the distance and knew the first waves of attacks were off. *Why are we not even in formation if they're launching the attack already?* He kicked his heels into his horse, urging a faster speed.

"Conton," he said, when he found the soldier. "Get everyone in formation. We need to prepare to flank the battle when Major Vosheim gives the order, understood?"

"Yes, sir!"

With Conton dispatched, Edelbrock examined the plains from horseback. The adjacent camp, where Major Sahl and his men had stayed, was now empty, their forces surging across the field. Two other groups—these weren't Calrym soldiers, but Remerian—joined Sahl on either side. They were led by Majors Burbaton and Stylos, two people Edelbrock hadn't met.

Further away, another group was doing the same as Edelbrock's. Forming up and getting ready to wait. That'd be Major Nuremlock's forces. Nuremlock, being a Calrite, was an officer Edelbrock was familiar with. Nuremlock was a stern, no-nonsense officer. Even the mere mention of Major Vosheim in his presence set his lip sneering. Edelbrock had reported to him once and, upon learning Edelbrock served under Vosheim, Nuremlock had become increasingly dismissive and agitated. Edelbrock didn't take it personally—he would've thought the same. He knew Nuremlock would pull off his flanking maneuver at the right time, as a genuine officer. Vosheim, however, was beginning to worry Edelbrock more, as he realized how far behind their orders had been.

His thoughts dissipated as he caught a glimpse through the marching army and saw the vast stretch of camels mounted by the nomads of Vessia. Rows of spear points stabbing the horizon caught his eye, and he swallowed. He remembered Jaylena and prayed to Mother Avani he'd make it through this. *Don't let me die. If I could just have one more day with my love... I'll do what's required to come out of this alive.* Edelbrock never considered himself a bad person, but he'd also come to terms with the fact that he'd do whatever it took to ensure his survival.

Then the army met the Camel Clans, and the morning turned into an epic clash of metal and beast, men, and wrath.

Time passed. Edelbrock waited on horseback. His thighs were stiff from clenching and his neck ached from craning in an attempt to see what was going on. But he couldn't see shit. He wished there were Magicai here to help. The Magicai, however, had been stationed in other areas, mostly defensively, in case the Camel Clans won the battle or had split their forces. They'd had a couple of Magicai earlier in the war, but the Camel Clans had focused on them with constant volleys of arrows. Their efforts were spent protecting themselves, and there weren't enough of them to go on the offensive. Several of them aged into death because they had to keep shielding themselves, doing nothing to hurt the Camel Clans. Edelbrock suspected many of them were inexperienced or junior Magicai. He wasn't sure how their organization worked, but he'd been less than impressed by them. He wondered if there was a reason they weren't out in stronger force and why Major Vosheim's battalion never had Magicai allies.

The sun rose higher. Edelbrock perspired. Everyone perspired. The stench of sweat and nervous piss eroded the distant scent of blood. Screams and shouts and moans could be heard. Scrapes and dings and smashes and rings. Edelbrock glanced over at Major Vosheim. Nothing. He looked further down the fields where Nuremlock and his men were. Also nothing.

Edelbrock wiped his sleepy eyes. He rolled a crisped bit of leftover sleep between his fingers, flicking it away, into the bloodied wind. Then, horns. Major Nuremlock and his men charging. He searched for Major Vosheim, spotted him sitting in his saddle, and picking his fingernails. *Apparently, the opportunity hasn't yet arisen.*

He heard whispers among the men. Dissension. Worry. Edelbrock should've stopped it, he knew, but he couldn't. He had those same worries. Major Vosheim was going to sit there, wait for victory, and claim prestigious awards and commendations for his part in the battle. It sickened Edelbrock. It sickened all his men, from what Edelbrock was hearing. They watched their comrades, their friends, their allies, die.

But there was nothing any of them could do. And then the wind picked up and dust and sand started pelting everyone and everything, and Edelbrock lost sight of the battle. Despite that, Major Vosheim still didn't act.

"Everyone's going to die, sir," Conton said at Edelbrock's side. Concern etched across Conton's face as he shielded his eyes from the swirling dirt. "What happens if they lose? We're going to face the surviving Camel Clans by ourselves? They'll slaughter us!"

"Keep your voice down, Corporal! Don't—" Edelbrock's mouth filled with grit and he coughed, spitting it out. "Don't alarm the men. Major Vosheim knows what he's doing." It pained him to say that. Conton knew it wasn't true. Edelbrock saw that. But, even worse, he saw Conton knew Edelbrock didn't think it was true.

"Sir," Conton said. He retreated from Edelbrock's horse, disappearing among the men.

Edelbrock swallowed a sudden need to vomit. He couldn't

let the soldiers see that. Then, after a few moments, he decided what needed doing.

"Conton!" The corporal reappeared. "I'm going to have words with Major Vosheim. We're either helping our fellow soldiers or..." he left the rest unsaid. He didn't know what he'd do. Didn't know what Conton would interpret that as. He realized he'd just implicated himself in war crimes without meaning to. He wasn't even sure what the unsaid part meant. *But we can't just sit here, an embarrassment.*

"Sir," Conton said, nodding. "We're with you." He clapped Edelbrock's lower back. "The men are with you."

Conton wasn't a legendary officer. He didn't have everyone in his pockets. Edelbrock knew Conton was just saying what he thought Edelbrock wanted to hear. Edelbrock smiled, nonetheless. "Thank you, Conton," he said. He wondered if it came to that what the men would do.

Edelbrock approached Major Vosheim, who was staring into the whipping sandstorm towards the battle.

"Captain," he said, without turning to greet Edelbrock.

"Sir."

"Is there a problem? We're to maintain our men until the opportunity for a flanking attack."

"That's why I'm here, sir," Edelbrock said. He cleared his throat, nervous, pausing for time. "Don't you think that time has come?"

"Captain," Major Vosheim said, shifting to meet Edelbrock's eyes. It probably would have been more intimidating if there weren't swirls of dirt and dust forcing them both to blink and squint and cover their eyes with their hands. "If you think we're going to charge into *that*," and he jerked his hand towards where the battle was, "you're out of your damn mind. The storm'll separate us as soon as we head in there. We won't be able to tell friend from foe. We don't even know *where* to attack."

"Yes, sir." The major had sound logic, of course. But still.

They'd had a job, the major had avoided doing it at the opportune time, and now they sat like children waiting for their fathers to return from battle. Edelbrock couldn't let it go. He'd never enjoyed authority being stupid. "We had an opportunity earlier. Sir."

Major Vosheim glared at Edelbrock. "Captain, if I want your fucking advice, I'll ask—"

Shouts from their soldiers interrupted the major, and Edelbrock and Vosheim looked up, confused by the noise. Edelbrock saw panicked faces, hands pointing, people yelling, hands tightening on weapons. Turning, Edelbrock saw camels walking their way. The Camel Clans had fought their way through the army. At a quick glance, Edelbrock surmised there was double their number. *So many.*

"Captain! Get the men ready for retreat!"

"What?" Edelbrock looked at the soldiers. Most stood there, looking up at the mounted officers, waiting for orders. They didn't have enough horses for half of their soldiers. They'd never outpace the camels. "We can't leave them to die, Major."

"I gave you an order, Captain!" Major Vosheim turned to the soldiers under his command. "Retreat! Run for your lives!"

The soldiers heard that and Edelbrock saw panic begin.

"Stand steady!" Edelbrock said.

Major Vosheim glared at him. His long hair swirled in the storm, and his hand reached down to his sword. "Are you disobeying me, Captain?"

"Sir." *Yes. Yes, I am.* Edelbrock drew his own sword. "I can't let this happen. You're getting everyone killed."

"I'm trying to save lives, Captain!" Major Vosheim drew his sword.

"Your own, maybe. But not anyone else's. Not theirs," he pointed at their soldiers, standing there without horses. "Not theirs," he pointed towards the battle, where the

Camel Clans crept ever closer. They were moving slowly, hesitant. As if they weren't expecting another group of armed men to be waiting for them. *As well, they shouldn't be. We should be in the fight by now.* "We don't have time for this, Major."

"Too true," he said. Major Vosheim thrust his blade at Edelbrock's gut.

Edelbrock leaned backward, parrying, but only just. Vosheim's sword grazed Edelbrock's side, cutting a gash across his hip.

Their blades clashed another couple of times before soldiers intervened.

Nobody touched Edelbrock, but Major Vosheim found himself pulled off his horse. A dozen blades penetrated his body in quick succession. Corporal Conton was one of them. Edelbrock shared a nod with the corporal, but there wasn't time for anything else. The Camel Clans were upon them.

"Form a line!" Edelbrock said, then his first foe was near. A spear thrust at his neck, but Edelbrock swept it away with his sword, cracking the wood. Then the rider rode past Edelbrock and a new enemy appeared in his place, this one wielding a scimitar.

Edelbrock lunged in his saddle, driving his blade into the rider's chest. He dropped the scimitar, slumped on his camel, and disappeared behind Edelbrock. Blood ran down his sword, its warmth dripping onto his hand. Wiping the blade off on his thigh, he waited for his next opponent. None came.

The Camel Clans had retreated. Or, as Edelbrock took in the blurry scenery, had stopped attacking. Rows of camels lined up, ready to attack.

The ring of combat slowed, then after several minutes, stopped.

Corporal Conton, blood streaking his forehead, approached Edelbrock's side. "We survived."

"That's because they were waiting, Conton."

"For what, sir?"

I have no clue. "Best guess? They were testing for a trap. The next push will be worse. They'll all be here." Edelbrock slid off the saddle and hit his horse on the rump, sending it away.

"What are you doing, sir?"

"There's no point in having one man on horseback. I'm an obvious target. Besides, I'm a soldier. Like you. Like all of us. It's too constricting, truth be told." Edelbrock felt more at home on the ground, where he'd been most of his soldiering life.

"Sir," Corporal Conton said, offering a grim smile. *Another dash of respect gained, I suppose.*

Edelbrock turned and faced the soldiers. "We need to stick together and hold the line—don't let them split us in half. Just hold and wait for reinforcements; the battle has to be over soon."

The familiar thundering of camel hooves steered Edelbrock's attention back towards the now-approaching enemy. He gripped his sword tighter in his fist and waited for them.

And then, chaos.

A row of camel warriors collided with the soldiers. Spears met flesh and dozens of Edelbrock's men fell. He deflected several spears himself, and then the warriors were leaping off the camels, engaging with scimitars as more of the camel riders filled the gaps they left as they died. Edelbrock could only see dust, metal, camels, and men—along with the odd female warrior in the Camel Clans ranks.

Blinking his way through another surge of the sandstorm, Edelbrock tried his best to parry the swords of two foes at once. He stumbled backwards, eyes watering and irritated from the dirt. He couldn't see. Waving his blade in front of him, attempting to guard himself while his other hand wiped at his face, he heard a death cry.

He blinked several more times, and through a watery veil, saw opponents lying dead at his feet and Corporal Conton standing in front of Edelbrock as his protector. Two more nomads had taken the place of their dead comrades and were now double-teaming Conton, one with a scimitar, the other thrusting at Conton with a spear.

Edelbrock snapped to action, leaping forward to assist the man who'd saved his life. He engaged the warrior wielding the scimitar, an ugly man with a lip curled in a permanent sneer because of a scar. He sidestepped a wide swing, closing the gap and plunged his sword into the ugly man's thigh. The nomad screamed, and Edelbrock withdrew the sword, stabbing the warrior again in the chest this time.

Conton had dispatched his opponent as well, but nursed an injured arm. It appeared as if the spear had connected.

"Thanks for saving my life."

Corporal Conton nodded, and then there were more nomads to fight.

Edelbrock and Conton dispatched each who took their fallen ally's place, at least five more times—*but who's counting?*—before a thrown spear took Conton in the throat. Choking, the corporal stumbled backward, the spear lodged in his throat, waving back and forth in the air.

"Fuck," Edelbrock said, catching him before he fell. Edelbrock eased Conton to the ground, laying him on the ground as gently as he could. Other Calrite soldiers swarmed around Edelbrock and Conton, forming a protective barrier around the injured corporal. "You're gonna be—" there was no point in finishing the sentence. Conton had already died.

Standing, Edelbrock surveyed the situation while he had a moment to breathe. He estimated half his force was gone, though it was difficult to tell with the sandstorm and the tangled mess of bodies—both living and dead—a battle always produced. They'd made a significant dent in the Camel Clan forces, but they were still outnumbered.

"Regroup!" Edelbrock shouted into the void. Nobody was going to hear him. He wasn't sure why bothered, but he yelled again anyway, just to feel like he was contributing something. "Regroup and reform!"

Two soldiers reported to him. Edelbrock sighed.

The protective barrier that'd been formed for Conton broke, and Edelbrock braced himself for the next attack.

He defeated two more foes before he heard Remerian horns. Edelbrock assumed it was Major Burbaton or Major Stylos regrouping from the battle. *Hopefully, they'll see us.*

He killed another nomad. Some asshole sat on their camel with a bow and arrow, loosing arrows at any open target. One of them was Edelbrock.

Edelbrock dove to the side as he saw the arrow coming, and it sank itself into a different soldier's chest under his command. The soldier died, and Edelbrock, for a moment, felt bad.

The camel sniper drew another arrow, and then collapsed, several arrows protruding from his back.

Remerian soldiers crashed into the pinned nomads and with renewed vigor, Edelbrock's battalion continued fighting.

The Camel Clansmen fought hard, but it didn't take long for them to perish once flanked. No prisoners were secured— the nomadic warriors fought to the death. *And we don't want prisoners, anyway.*

A regal-looking man on horseback approached Edelbrock and the surrounding soldiers.

He had a stiff voice, a stiffer jaw, and a clean-shaven face. In another world, perhaps, Edelbrock may have found the man handsome.

"This must be Major Vosheim's heroic force, eh?" the man asked with a more charming voice than Edelbrock would've presumed the man would have. He smiled at a few of his own soldiers and they chuckled. Edelbrock noticed the man's teeth were perfect, aside from a gap—he was missing one of his canines. On his breast, Edelbrock caught sight of a medal marking him as a major.

"Major," Edelbrock said. "I'm Captain Edelbrock Brendis. You're correct. This is—was—Major Vosheim's force. He's dead, sir." *Dead because we murdered him.*

"Dead?" Major Mystery asked. "Explain dead. Because the Major Vosheim *I* know wouldn't have perished in any bout of combat. I'm astounded you're not halfway to the Calrite capital, tails tucked between your legs." He flashed his charming grin again and his soldiers laughed again. *He is a charming fellow.*

"Sir," Edelbrock said. *What the fuck do I say? We'll be executed for treason.* He wondered if that was true. Instead of fleeing, they'd held the line and fought. That had to earn some favor, right? "He commanded a retreat."

"Might I remind you that you're addressing a major in the Remerian army?" Major Mystery pointed at the medal on his chest. "Enough delaying, Captain. Out with the truth."

"We killed him." Edelbrock paused, realizing he'd just implicated the entire regiment. "I killed him, sir. Couldn't let that stand. We were needed here."

Major Mystery frowned. "Who's in charge now? You, Captain?"

Edelbrock shrugged. "Only be default, sir. But considering the circumstances, I assume I should stand down." This had been the gamble he'd taken by standing up to Major Vosheim. But he'd taken a gamble knowingly. No loyal soldier would stand for desertion, no matter how esteemed an officer they were. And anybody of importance didn't consider Major Vosheim esteemed by any stretch, in Edelbrock's estimation.

"That's not up to me, Captain. I'm from Remeria and I don't give a shit what you do in Calrym." Major Mystery hopped off the horse, handing the reins to a nearby soldier, then approached Edelbrock. "I'm Major Kelst Burbaton."

"Sir, you're a legend." That wasn't true, but he figured a bit of flattery didn't hurt anyone. He was, in any case, about to become a legend. Edelbrock had seen no other important surviving officers.

"I'm no legend, Captain, but I appreciate the flattery." Major Burbaton grinned, then turned to look at the weary soldiers Edelbrock had been fighting alongside. "Don't look so gloomy," he said. "We won the battle. The Camel Clans are dead or retreated."

The soldiers cheered, and a wave of relief brushed through Edelbrock.

"Walk with me, Captain."

Edelbrock walked alongside Major Burbaton until they'd made their way to the perimeter of soldiers. He saw other remnants of soldiers and noticed the sandstorm was waning.

"I have unfortunate news," Major Burbaton said. "Major Sahl perished in battle. Major Nuremlock as well."

That was the three highest ranking officers deployed in this battle, dead, including Vosheim. "And Major Stylos, sir?" Edelbrock didn't care about Major Stylos—another Remerian officer—but he felt inclined to inquire out of politeness.

Major Burbaton snorted. "Major Stylos was the *actual* hero in this battle, son." Edelbrock didn't like being called that. He doubted this Burbaton fellow was more than two or three years older than him. "He's giving chase to the few enemy soldiers who fled, though Mother Avani knows why. A few dozen soldiers won't do much."

Edelbrock caught himself examining how proportionate Major Burbaton's nose was, and wondered why. *A strange detail to notice.* He realized he'd done the same thing when examining Jaylena back home.

"In any case, Captain, I appreciate what you did. You stood up to an officer—not a straightforward affair. If you had retreated, my men and I would've had to fight the battle. And, from what I saw, the enemy doubled your number. You were, frankly, about to lose. However, if you didn't remain on the battlefield, my force would have been outnumbered, and with no reinforcements to save us. You did a great thing, soldier." Major Burbaton held his hand out to shake Edelbrock's. Edelbrock accepted it.

"Thank you, sir."

"I have no issue writing forth a recommendation to the Calrite leadership, outlining your excellent tactics and heroic actions, with maybe a bit of … flair, to make it sound better." Major Burbaton smirked. "There's nothing wrong with a bit of embellishment, not when you've won the war. You deserve it, hero. Maybe you'll even earn a promotion out of it. Make yourself a real career, a respectable man. Find yourself a pretty woman to marry. Just don't make the same mistake Vosheim did, and you'll not find a knife in your back. Trust is an important thing, Captain, and the moment you breach it, somebody's going to capitalize upon it."

Sometime after his promotion to the rank of major, the defeat of a second wave of Camel Clan invaders, and his return to Lochwall—whereupon he married Jaylena and secured a position as a minor nobleman—he'd come to regret not taking Major Burbaton's warning to heart.

Hiding in Plain Sight

Divinius Murdlow shivered. The frigid ocean breeze which consistently tore through the port town of Coldridge, froze everything and everyone. Divinius, a well-respected business owner, pulled his expensive fur cloak tight. Beneath the cloak, his tailored clothing seemed to stick to his skin, stretching and stiffening against the chill. He picked up his pace, although it wasn't as fast as he may have liked—he'd gained a decent amount of weight since achieving success.

He waddled—unfortunately, that's where he was now—down the snow-covered streets, passing a few homeless people huddled against the rear of his tavern, Lezlie's Plaice. Divinius ignored the leeches. They didn't cause any harm and were seeking a bit of warmth. The fireplace happened to be on that wall, and Divinius knew it shielded much of the freezing wind. He didn't allow them inside Lezlie's Plaice—paying customers only—but he wasn't as strict as other business owners. Perhaps he had a soft heart. Perhaps he knew what their plight was. Divinius shook such thoughts from his head. He wasn't that identity anymore. He was a respectable businessman, and he needed to act like one—not like a poor, desperate man.

Stepping through the door to Lezlie's Plaice, Divinius was assaulted by an oppressive heat. That was normal in Cyrok. The winter's cold seeped into buildings, and the only way to combat it was to keep a fire burning hot. He glanced around the large room, noticing plenty of empty tables and an eerie quiet. The two or three patrons weren't socializing, and the barkeep, Lezlie, seemed preoccupied with stirring a cauldron. He smiled upon seeing her curly blonde hair.

Lezlie had owned the tavern before he'd purchased it. Behind on her payments, Lezlie needed a way out. Divinius offered her a deal—he bought the establishment, kept her old name, kept her on to run it, and they split the profits after business expenses. A great deal for Lezlie, not so great a deal for Divinius. However, with his reputation suffering in Coldridge, he'd needed to do something to make reparations. The townspeople loved Lezlie, and her backing had withheld their dislike of Divinius. For a while, anyway.

Simply put, Divinius had come in too hot. He'd arrived in Coldridge two years ago with a lot of money and even more ego. With that money, he bought out respected businesses. And, in the early days, he wasn't afraid of doing some horrible things to the previous owners.

Needless to say, Divinius had screwed up.

He approached the bar, the familiar smell of boiled plaice touching his nose. "Again?" he asked, his breath an asthmatic wheezing from exerting his body too much.

Lezlie turned and grinned. "Aye, again." Her expression melted into a sad one before her cheery disposition returned. "Still waiting for a shipment of venison to arrive."

His mouth watered at the sound of that. In the middle of winter, trade in Cyrok slowed, dependent on the weather. And the last few weeks had been brutal, with serious snow and freezing temperatures a regularity.

"I'm sick of plaice."

"I know," she said.

"What's in the cauldron?" He knew the boiled fish smell came from the kitchens. The cauldron was generally a stew or soup of some sort, and he hoped it wasn't of a fish's variety.

She grimaced, and he knew the answer wouldn't be to his liking. "Plaice stew."

He winced. "Of course. Always fish something. And lately, seems to be plaice."

"The catch has struggled to yield anything lately. The fishers are unloading their frozen stock. And right now, that's plaice. I can only sell what I find at the market, Divvy. You know that."

He snorted, annoyed, but unable to argue with that logic. He also noticed her purposeful usage of the nickname she'd given him when he'd offered her the business deal of a lifetime. Letting it slide at the time seemed a friendly gesture. Now it'd become permanent.

"You still want it though, don'tcha?" Lezlie asked.

Divinius nodded. He was starving and needed to eat something.

"Ale?"

"Of course." He rubbed his girth, attempting to slow his breathing enough to stop the wheezing. Winter always bothered him.

Lezlie served him a bowl of plaice stew and a tankard of ale. He consumed both in silence, reminiscing over the days when Lezlie's Plaice was packed. But now it was winter and people were hibernating, sheltering from the cold. He thought about the homeless people, and how much of a shame it was they were outside, shivering, when they could be in here, warm. They didn't have money though, and he couldn't support leeches. And they drove proper business away. It wasn't a coldhearted decision; it was a financial one. He'd learned long ago that surviving this harsh world started with being wealthy.

The front door opened, then closed. A shifty-looking fellow weaseled his way over to the bar and sat next to Divinius.

Bartrem. Great. Bartrem was a spy, but not a very good one. Everyone knew he was a spy, and he worked for nobody in particular. He'd approach people with potential information, and you could either pay him a coin or tell him to go away. Most of the time, his "information" was commonsense bullshit everyone already knew.

"I'm frozed like an icicle."

Divinius grunted. His left hand went into his cloak pocket, and he felt the familiar ice-cold metal of the coins he kept in his pocket. There was something about feeling money Divinius always enjoyed. Some might even say he obsessed. Perhaps it was his success as a businessman. Perhaps it was because in another life, he wasn't a rich, and wouldn't have access to it. He wasn't sure, but he enjoyed its reassurance.

"Got information," Bartrem said.

"Sure you do."

"I'm serious. Lezlie, a pint, please. I'm sure Divvy won't mind after he hears what I gots for him."

Divinius clapped Bartrem on the backside of his head. "Don't call me that."

"Aw, damn, it was a joke," Bartrem said, rubbing his head. "I can still get the pint, though, right? I swear, you need this information."

Lezlie picked a glass up, preparing to fill it.

"No," Divinius said. "He's as much a leech as the ones outside. Get out or buy something."

She filled the glass anyway and downed it herself. *Good ol' Lezlie.*

"Aw, c'mon, sir. I don't have any money."

"Yes, that's the problem." Divinius took a moment to

inhale, then exhale. He wanted to maintain his composure. His fingers selected a coin in his pocket, flipping one around in his hand. *Calm yourself.*

"It's a matter of life and death, Mr. Murdlow," Bartrem said. He had a serious look on his face. Something Divinius had never seen before.

"Fine. Go ahead, Lezlie, give him *one.*"

Lezlie filled a pint with Bartrem's preferred brand of whiskey. After sliding it over to Bartrem, Lezlie refilled her pint and downed that one, too. *It's a wonder she's not drunk all the time.*

"Many thanks, many thanks," Bartrem said. He emptied the pint, coughed once, grinned, and set the glass down—a bit too roughly, for a free drink, if Divinius had a say about it.

"What's this news, then?" Divinius asked.

"It's bad. Real bad. But I'm cold, Mr. Murdlow. One more, please? Then we must go somewhere private."

"Fine." Divinius never put up with Bartrem's act, but something felt different today. Bartrem was being too serious.

Bartrem downed a second pint of whiskey, smacking his lips. "Splendid stuff, splendid. Need to come around more often, I thinks. Need to come around more often, for sure."

"Perhaps with money on hand, next time," Divinius said. "Let's go." He heaved himself off the stool, and the wheezing returned. "Damn cold, makes breathing near impossible."

"Better get used to it," Bartrem said. "Better get used to it, indeed. Quick, now, Mr. Murdlow. No time to waste."

Two rooms flanked the huge common area in Lezlie's Plaice—the first, a private dining area for prestigious guests or a place to conduct meetings, and the second, a hall which led to a stairwell that went to the second floor where all the rented rooms were. Bartrem, obviously unfamiliar with the establishment's other rooms, headed to the stairwell. "No," Divinius wheezed, "this way." He brought Bartrem into the private dining room.

As soon as the door closed, Bartrem launched into a typical Bartrem speech. "Mr. Murdlow, the information I bring is valuable. Very valuable, yes. I would think some sort of advance payment would be advisable considering how important said news is to you. Now, if—"

Divinius grabbed hold of Bartrem's clothes, yanking him closer. "Tell me what you know and if it's worth it, you'll get your money. But stop stalling."

Bartrem gulped, nodding vigorously. "I understand."

"Then what is it?"

"The Falcon Knights have launched a formal warrant for your arrest just before I came in here. They want—"

"Fuck," Divinius said, tossing Bartrem to the ground. He didn't need to hear anything else. He reached into his pocket, grabbed the handful of coins, and threw them after the retreating Bartrem.

He waddled back to the bar, where Lezlie was cleaning the glasses they'd left behind. "Lezlie."

She looked up, offering a kind smile. "Aye."

"The tavern is yours." He reached into another pocket, retrieving another handful of coins, and dropped them on the bar. "And money. You don't know where I am. I've appreciated our partnership, but I need to disappear. I'll leave some stuff on my bed, in my room. If you could be so kind as to burn them when I leave."

"Aye," she said. She filled a pint. "One for the road?"

Divinius snorted. It was the shit Bartrem drank. The stuff Divinius never touched. But he didn't have to be Divinius anymore. "Sure," he said, taking it and tossing it back. "Thanks, Lezlie."

"You'll always have a place here, Divvy. Good luck with… whatever's going on."

He nodded, then waddled away, hurrying to the staircase. Lezlie was a good woman. A good person. He'd told her long ago that he might have to disappear one day. Today was that day. As soon as he was out of earshot, he stopped his wheezing and picked up his pace. He entered his room, locking the door behind him.

Divinius gathered his belongings, throwing them on the bed. He stripped off his clothes and removed the contraption he'd worn to increase his bulk. Now, thirty pounds smaller around the waist, he'd look a fair bit different. He sighed, knowing what his new identity had to be.

As he considered a new name, he searched through his belongings, finding the tattered clothing he searched for. Old traveling clothes he'd worn, scuffed up, and colors fading from use. He slipped those on, then found a piece of charcoal he'd kept with him, smearing his hands and face in ash. Being a wealthy businessman, he'd kept a clean-cut appearance. Now he needed to disappear. Smearing glue across his chin and cheeks, he placed a fake beard made from wool and dyed a dark brown on his face. He rubbed the charcoal in the too-clean beard and practiced a sickly cough. He tried low-sounding coughs, and high ones, he tried a hacking one, and he even gathered saliva in his mouth to produce a wet spatter when he coughed.

He used a small knife to cut bunches of hair from his head, ruffled the remaining hair around, and rubbed the charcoal through it, as well. He stuffed the cut hair in a small pouch and shoved that in a pocket. Then he pulled his hood up, ensuring his beard didn't shift when he did so.

Satisfied with his quick performance, he retrieved a walking stick he'd found on his journey to Coldridge, and rubbed the charcoal over that, too. He practiced hunching and walking with a limp.

And then he left all his belongings on the bed. Left his money on a side table for Lezlie. She deserved it, and he wouldn't need it anymore. He wasn't a rich businessman. Divinius Murdlow was dead.

Crouching, he used the walking stick like a cane and

limped his way out of the room. He descended the stairs and crossed the common room to the fireplace, and tossed the pouch of cut hair in. He watched it burn and felt warmth flow through him. Lezlie wasn't at the bar, and what few patrons there were gave him strange looks. He suppressed a grin, realizing it was working.

"You shouldn't be here," a patron said. "You'll get thrown out."

He nodded. Then, in a raspy voice, he said, "Thanks." Voices were something he practiced often because it was a skill which needed maintenance to keep.

Shuffling out the door of Lezlie's Plaice, he almost felt sad to leave. He went behind the establishment, saw the three homeless vagrants huddling together against the cold, and limped over. They accepted him, and then there were four homeless vagrants huddling together against the cold, hoping the fire inside Lezlie's Plaice would burn just a little hotter, so they could feel just a little warmer.

The evening faded into night, and the Falcon Knights seemed to be in a hurry to find him. They ran back and forth, ignoring him. He was sure they'd figured out his former identity—that of a criminal. *Who am I kidding?* He snorted. Almost every identity he'd held had been criminal for one reason or another.

A scuffle broke the quiet, cold air, and he peered through a crack in the bodies to observe. The familiar sound of metal ringing from a sword being drawn rang out, followed by a cry for help. He swore he heard the gush of a blade plunging into flesh, before another cry followed the previous, though this one was full of agony and pain. He saw a group of Falcon Knights walking away from a body tossed onto the cold ground.

When the knights disappeared around a building, he removed himself from the huddled vagrants. Reaching the slaughtered person, it took only a moment for him to recognize its identity—Bartrem. The unfortunate spy—if one could even call him that—lay in a pool of blood. He recognized not one, but two stab wounds in Bartrem's chest. Bartrem's mouth hung open, a drool of red sliding from his mouth, joining the puddle forming from his eviscerated abdomen.

"Some men get what they deserve." He wasn't one of them. Not yet, at least.

He decided it was time to begin his journey away from Coldridge. He turned from Bartrem's corpse and started limping. Time to put on a new person—one whom the soldiers wouldn't enjoy being around if they approached him.

It wasn't long before he ran into a pair of Falcon Knights holding torches in the middle of their search patrol.

"Hold," one of them said. "Who are you?" The Falcon Knight lowered the torch, shining the light into the hood and onto the fake beard.

"Just a man out for a piss," he said.

"We're on the lookout for a criminal businessman. His name is Divinius Murdlow. Perhaps you've seen him in hiding? He's a heavier fellow, clean shaven, owns several buildings in this town."

He shook his head. "Haven't seen him."

"But you know of him?" the Falcon Knight pressed.

"Everyone in this town has heard of that greasy bastard," he said, spitting in the snow. Divinius had never been greasy, but he knew the insult would provide the Falcon Knights with two pieces of information. The first, that he clearly had never seen Divinius in person. And the second—even if he *knew* Divinius, he obviously didn't like the man.

"Right. What's your name?"

He looked up, past the torchlight, meeting the Falcon Knight's eyes. He hawked some phlegm up, chewed it for a moment, and spat it in between the soldier's boots. Then he shoved a pinky in his nose, swirled it around to collect its contents, and wiped it on his cloak. Disgusted, the Falcon Knight took a step back.

"The name's Vithor Bane," he said. "And unless you need anything further, I have somewhere to be."

They let him go. Thoughts of poor Bartrem's fate followed him, and he breathed a sigh of relief—the birth of Vithor Bane, his new persona, was a grand success.

MARBLES

Some people called Tevin Whitestar dumb because he couldn't speak. Others called him mute. Still others thought him incapable of doing simple things. He wasn't stupid. He could understand and communicate with anyone willing to be patient and read his chalkboard or sign with him. Most people, Tevin had noticed, lacked patience. And often the people who lacked patience tended to be the worst behaved.

At twelve years old, Tevin looked like he was probably nine. He was small for his age. Smaller still when standing next to his best friend, Bendicio Flokes, though everyone just called him by his last name. Both their parents were stevedores who never seemed to leave the docks of Bryn. Tevin's parents, he was pretty sure, found Flokes to be a blessing because the much larger boy took care of Tevin. Protected him. Had Flokes not been around, Tevin would be a much bigger burden on his parents. They'd want to find somebody to care for him from the other kids. He knew that.

Tevin carried his chalkboard in one hand, even though his father had drilled a hole through it and looped a piece of rope so Tevin could carry it over his shoulder if he wished. A small pouch on his belt held a variety of chalk sticks. Sometimes, when he was feeling rebellious, he and Flokes would use the chalk on the deserted alleys, drawing and writing scandalous things. His parents would, of course, be furious if they knew. They worked too hard for him to waste that chalk. He knew it. But, even knowing it, sometimes Tevin felt the need to have a bit of fun.

Flokes was leaning against the side of a building, watching the passersby. "I'm bored," he said, whining.

Tevin was bored, too. When they weren't aiding the various businesses that paid them to do the odd chore, they found themselves alone and wondering what to do. The older they became, the more frequently it seemed they found themselves bored. Tevin pulled out chalk, writing on his board. *Want to write on some buildings with chalk?* He flipped the chalkboard over, showing Flokes.

His friend read it. "No. We've already drawn everything there is to draw, Tev. Written everything there is to write. There must be something else."

Tevin used the sleeve of his shirt to wipe the chalk from the board. *Marbles?* he wrote, flipping the board over again.

Flokes shrugged. "We could. Not against each other, though. We could go down to Dockpoint Alley and gamble on a match."

Dockpoint Alley was the closest alley to the docks. It was also the most direct route there, outside of the main road, which was always cluttered with traffic, carts, goods being loaded and unloaded, and guard patrols. The road had a real name, something boring, like Perth Street. Tevin couldn't remember because nobody called it that. The problem with Dockpoint Alley was it had become the main hangout place for Snarls and his gang. Snarls was a few years older than Tevin, and it was no mystery why everyone called him "Snarls". The boy was mean, and Tevin didn't like the idea of playing marbles with him.

Why? Snarls is there.

"Snarls?" Flokes shrugged again. "You worry too much, Tev. Kid's more bark than bite. Besides, if he tries anything, I'll be there." Flokes stood straighter, pulling away from the building he leaned against to flex his muscles easier.

He has a whole gang.

"Yeah, I know, but they're nothing. Trust me. I just played marbles with him the other day."

But you're awful. I bet he won.

Flokes sighed. "Yes, he did." After a moment, he shrugged, like he was admitting to a crime. "I lost a lot of money," he mumbled.

Tevin arched a brow at that. *If I play him, I'll win.*

"You can bet the small amount we have, and we'll have enough to do something fun, Tev."

You can't be serious. He'll kill us before he lets us win. Tevin knew Snarls. The boy was greedy, arrogant, and a bully. He wouldn't let Tevin of all people best him at marbles, and even if he did, he wouldn't let Tevin walk away with the spoils of winning.

"He'll honor the bet. He'll have to. Otherwise, he'll lose all credibility. Don't lose your marbles. The girls won't like that." Flokes grinned and chuckled.

Tevin didn't think so. Snarls was the head of the controlling gang of young adults that roamed the town. The only people who could stand up to Snarls and his cronies were adults, and most of them were intimidated. The town guard and other criminals were about the only ones who didn't bend the knee to the gang known as the Dockpoint Daggers. As far as Tevin knew, the Dockpoint Daggers hadn't committed any serious crimes, but he expected that to change any moment now. The last time he'd seen them, they seemed antsy and anxious, and Tevin had overheard one of Snarls's goons talking about stabbing somebody for fun. Tevin didn't want that somebody to be him.

Can't we play somebody else?

"Nobody else is going to go against you for money with marbles, Tev. You're good. Too good. Snarls is good. It'll be a decent match he'll feel challenged in, but I know you'll win. He'll have to pay. I bet he even gets a kick out of losing."

Tevin reached down and fumbled with the pouch of marbles hanging from his belt. They clinked and clattered, and he smiled. He liked his marbles, the way they felt, the variety of colors. Sometimes he'd just hold one—usually his favorite, the lighter blue one with speckles of black—and twirl it around in his fingers, feeling the smooth exterior roll around his skin.

His mind returned to thoughts of Snarls and the Dockpoint Daggers. Would they hurt Tevin Whitestar? He looked like a child, and even at twelve, would they harm him? Snarls was at least sixteen, if not older. He couldn't hurt a kid… right? Tevin's intuition fought against the direction his mind was taking. *No, if Snarls thought he needed to, he'd kill a baby.*

"Come on, Tev."

Flokes led the way to Dockpoint Alley. They weaved through a few crowds before slipping into the quieter street. Dockpoint Alley found itself sandwiched between several tall and thick buildings, which prevented a lot of the city noise from entering. It felt, Tevin often thought, like Snarls and his gang could murder him and no matter how loud his screams became, nobody would hear him. The building insulated Dockpoint Alley, creating a sort of isolated pathway. Perhaps that's why Snarls and the Dockpoint Daggers preferred it here.

A wall of old, rotting crates met them just inside Dockpoint Alley. The Dockpoint Daggers had moved these crates here to create a barrier between the alleyway and the rest of Bryn. Two hulking figures leaned against the crates, eyeing Flokes and Tevin as they approached.

"Flokes? Back for another round of marbles?" one asked. The other chuckled.

"Fuck off, Phlegm. Move. My friend Tev here is going to beat Snarls at marbles, win some money for us."

The gang members both laughed. The one Flokes called Phlegm snorted and hawked a glob of snot onto the stone road. "Fine. Good luck," Phlegm said.

Flokes and Tevin slipped through the opening in the rotting crates and plunged into darkness. Tevin could see, but faintly. The tall buildings blocked much of the sunlight, and the crates piled up at both ends of Dockpoint Alley didn't help. The first time Tevin had entered the alley, he'd been so worried nobody could read his chalkboard. That didn't happen. Tevin also would've expected Snarls to be an absolute ass regarding the chalkboard, and Tevin's inability to speak, but somehow, that wasn't the case with Snarls—he was a prick, but not about that. A few flickering lights caught Tevin's attention—torches lit in the daytime. Seemed odd, as the Dockpoint Daggers preferred it darker.

They passed several small crowds of Dockpoint Daggers as they came to the midpoint of Dockpoint Alley. Tevin saw plenty of small daggers and knives on belts. The arid smell of skachi smoke met his nostrils. He hated the smell. His father smoked the stuff, and it always made him cough. He coughed, then rolled his eyes, sighing in acceptance. The skachi was new to Dockpoint Alley, as far as Tevin knew.

Tevin spotted Snarls. Keithan "Snarls" Stonebark cut an imposing figure compared to the other thugs of the Dock-point Daggers. Snarls was as wide as he was tall, a giant of a person, looming over everyone. Tevin recalled Snarls used to be pure muscle, but laziness and making usage of his cronies had allowed Snarls to fatten up, losing much of the toned figure he'd once possessed. He turned, glancing at both Flokes and Tevin, and offered one of his infamous snarls, lip raising up enough for his yellowed teeth to show.

"Snarls," Flokes said.

Snarls held up a hand. "No, Bendicio, no," he said. He used Flokes's first name, because Snarls didn't call anyone by their nickname. He'd once said, "It built camaraderie, and I'm not here to make friends. I'm here to make money." Snarls reached into a pocket, pulling out a rolled skachi leaf. He placed it in his mouth and leaned toward a torch, letting the leaf catch aflame. Puffing, he reached up, pulling the leaf from his mouth and flicking ashes on the ground. Tevin understood the need for the daytime torches. "Call me by my real name now, Bendicio. I'm a man growed. No need for childhood nicknames. Keithan it is."

"Keithan," Flokes said. Tevin heard the annoyance in his voice, but doubted Snarls would catch it. Most people didn't realize when Flokes was annoyed until he swung a fist at them.

"Tevin, right?" Snarls asked.

Tevin nodded.

"I remember you."

"He's looking to challenge you to a match of marbles, Keithan."

"Is that right, Bendicio? Can't win yourself so you dragged this child with you? Think he's gonna win some-hows?" Snarls laughed, then caught a plume of the smoke and started coughing, a great hacking cough, like one Tevin's father would issue.

Flokes waited for Snarls to stop coughing before speaking. "I think he could beat you, Keithan. He beats me regularly."

"Everyone in Bryn beats you at marbles, Bendicio," Snarls said, taking another drag of the skachi leaf. He exhaled, smoke spilling from his nostrils. "Let's say I agree to a match. What're the stakes?"

"Money."

"I figured that, but how much?"

Flokes drew out his money, while Tevin handed over the

small amount he had. Together, they had a pitiful amount. Tevin knew a stevedore earned more in a single day's work. But it was all they had.

Snarls looked at the small amount of coin in Flokes's hand. "Seriously? It's not even worth drawin' the Xs on the ground for that much, Bendicio. Get outta here, before I find you insulting."

Tevin frowned before writing on his chalkboard. *What about my collection of marbles? You win, you can have them all. Except for my shooter.* Tevin wouldn't risk trading his favorite marble.

Snarls shook his head. "Got plenty of me own marbles."

"But you don't have Tevin's marbles," Flokes said. "He's got some beauties."

"Let's see 'em, then," Snarls said.

Tevin emptied his marble pouch into his hand. The torchlight reflected off the various colors. Most people in Bryn had bland designs. Tevin wasn't sure where his collection had come from, but they'd always impressed the people he played against.

"Them's are gorgeous," Snarls said, inhaling deep. He coughed again, then dropped the leaf and stamped it out with a boot. Tevin wondered if he was coughing because he wasn't yet used to the skachi. "Yeah, that'll do. Draw the Xs."

Tevin smiled and handed a stick of chalk to Flokes. Flokes was much better at drawing straight lines than Tevin was.

Marbles was a simple game. It could be played nearly anywhere, as long as one had marbles and some way of marking a few spots on the ground. All it took was two Xs drawn in the dirt or on the ground with chalk. They would then place a colored marble on each of the four ends of the X, with a black marble placed in the middle of the X. The two players would take their spots at a measured spot away from the X—in a standard game of marbles, this would be two feet from the X—and alternate turns tossing or rolling other marbles at their opponent's marbles. The aim was to knock their opponent's colored marbles off their starting positions so they no longer touched any part of the X without touching the black marble. Once the four marbles were displaced, they had to hit the black marble off its spot. If one could knock the black marble onto one of the four starting positions, that was called a "double win" and the winner received double their bet.

"All right," Flokes said, tossing the chalk back to Tevin, "it's done."

Snarls took a glance at the two Xs, nodded. "Looks fair to me."

"Tev?" Flokes asked.

It was customary for both opponents to agree to the setup before beginning the match. Tevin knew Flokes wouldn't mess it up, but looked anyway, then nodded.

"Good." Snarls hefted a pouch in his hand. "Then let's place our marbles, eh? Not trying to waste all day on this. Hardly worth bothering, really. But I admit, your marbles are pretty 'nuff to wager a few coins, and there's not much else happening round these parts at the moment."

Tevin handed his chalkboard to Flokes—a measure of trust, as he didn't like not having his chalkboard on hand— and selected the jet black marble he had in his collection, placing it on the axis of the X. Then he moved to each of the four ends of the chalk marking, selecting a colored marble and placing it on the ground. Tevin picked these colors to distract Snarls during the game. He hoped the vibrant colors and designs would throw Snarls off. The first was a bright ruby with gold flecks dotted throughout, the second an emerald-sapphire swirl, the third a deep purple with yellow stars, and the fourth was an array of bright colors all glimmering against the backdrop of silver—maybe his most eye-catching marble. He found his shooter, the light blue marble with speckles of black, and held it in his fist, making his way back over to Flokes.

Snarls was already done setting his marbles, taking much less care in his selection than Tevin had his. He had a new leaf of skachi lit and in-between his teeth, puffing away. Tevin glanced at the other X, four bland, plain blue marbles placed at each end of the X.

"Now," Snarls said, breathing out a breath of the pungent skachi odor. "The stakes: I win, I keep this money," he rattled his hand, and the coins chinked against one another. "And," he nodded at Tevin, eyes on the pouch hanging from Tevin's belt, "thems there marbles. You win, you triple your coin. Fair?"

"Fair," Flokes said, as Tevin nodded.

"Ready to begin?" Snarls asked.

Tevin nodded.

"Good. You shoot first."

There was no significant advantage to going first in marbles. Snarls likely wanted to size Tevin up, see what he was up against.

Tevin opened his hand, looking at his favorite marble. He approached his opponent's X, stepping up to the line Flokes had drawn two feet away. He examined the four plain blue marbles, the black one in the center, spinning his shooting marble around in his hand as he readied himself for the first shot.

He let the marble roll into his fingers, allowing it to rest on at the end of his fore-and-middle fingers, then flicked his thumb. The marble skipped off his hand, landing on the street, and clashed into his target, removing the blue marble from its place. Tevin pumped a fist in the air, then retrieved both the shooting marble and the marble he'd displaced.

"Not bad," Snarls said, flicking the skachi leaf to the ground again, and stomping it out.

Tevin noticed others had joined them now, watching the

game. All Dockpoint Daggers, of course. Tevin glanced at Flokes, but he seemed unconcerned. Flokes rarely noticed when he should be concerned, though.

Snarls stepped up to the X, holding Tevin's marbles. Instead of flicking his shot like most marbles players, Snarls swung his arm back, then let it go. The marble dropped from his hand, rolling and bouncing along the road. It met its mark, though, and Tevin watched as the emerald-sapphire swirl marble was knocked from its place.

Tevin took his turn, displacing a second marble from the X. Likewise, Snarls knocked the ruby marble with gold flecks off its spot.

He needed to do something clever if he was going to win against Snarls. Tevin could tell Snarls was skillful. He bet if they kept doing this, they'd tie several games before a winner was declared. But Tevin wanted to win. He considered his options. He could try to knock the last two marbles off at once, as they did line up. Or perhaps win by knocking the black marble onto one of the other marbles' starting positions —a much more difficult task.

Tevin took aim, flicked the marble harder than before. The marble left his hand, shooting down the road, clashing into its target. The displaced marble jolted forwards, clinking off the side of Tevin's secondary target, and coming to a halt. *Damn.* The second marble had only shifted for a mere moment before tipping back to its original place.

"That was close," Snarls said. "This boy is good, Bendicio."

Flokes snorted. "He is. Beats me every time I play him."

"Everybody does." Snarls rolled his marble. It clinked across the stone and caught in a small crack, shifting its direction. The marble just touched his target before stopping. "Are you fucking kidding me? Did you see that?" When nobody answered, Snarls stomped his foot. "Did you fucking see that?"

Tevin nodded, and other Dockpoint Dagger members shouted their agreement.

Snarls turned to Flokes. "You set this up. You fucked me on purpose!"

Flokes, stunned, stared at Snarls. Tevin felt numb.

"You rigged it. I knew I couldn't trust you. You're still angry I beat you at marbles, you're already well awares of the fact I'm the best marbles player in this whole town. So you set me up, Bendicio. You set Keithan Stonebark up. I don't like being set up, Bendicio!" Snarls stomped over to the X, kicking the black marble off its spot. "Convenient," he said. "I just won!" He stooped over, scooping the marbles up in his hand, then turned to Tevin. "Give me the rest, like you promised."

"That's no fair," Flokes said. "You didn't finish the game properly. We don't owe you anything."

Tevin shook his head no, but Flokes didn't notice him. He was too enraged by Snarls. Tevin hurried over to Flokes, ripping the chalkboard from his grasp. *No!* he wrote, waving the board in front of Flokes's face.

Flokes read it, gnashed his teeth, then shoved the chalkboard—and Tevin—out of his way. He surged toward Snarls. "You're a cheat and a scoundrel. A bloody criminal who's too afraid to take on a child. What's the matter? You thought you were gonna lose, eh? Fucking pathetic, you are. Dockpoint Daggers?" Flokes laughed. "Pathetic, all of you. Doubt any of you have ever even used a dagger, you lousy pretenders. Give Tevin back his marbles, or I'll go get the town guard. See how tough you are then, you bastard."

What are you doing? You're going to get us killed! But Flokes ignored the writing. Tevin wished he could scream, but he couldn't make any sounds. He grit his teeth, frustrated tears welling up in his eyes. And now, in order to walk out of Dockpoint Alley alive, he was going to lose his marbles, too. He pocketed his shooter, the light blue marble with the black speckles, and removed the pouch of his remaining marbles from his belt.

"You're being cockier than I'd have thought, Bendicio," Snarls said. He reached behind his back, and when his hand came back into view, Tevin noticed he held a long, curved blade. "You don't know what we are capable of. The Dockpoint Daggers aren't afraid of a petch… a petalant? No… a…" Snarls stopped a moment. "A disobedient child. Say one more thing I don't like and I'll make sure you don't walk out of here with your stomach intact."

"You're pathetic," Flokes said. "Come on, Tevin."

It's okay, I'll give. Tevin didn't get through the rest of the sentence before he heard Flokes scream out. He looked over and Snarls was plunging his blade into Flokes again.

"Tevin," Flokes managed to blurt before the blade bit into his skin again. He cried out, holding his arms up in a defensive position. The blade slashed a finger from his left hand and he yelled again, blood running down his arm, dripping on the stone road. "Run!" Tevin noticed blood frothing from Flokes's mouth and he gaped in horror. "Run!" The blade sank into his side and Flokes collapsed.

Tevin looked around, noticed a gap between two Dockpoint Daggers men, and ducked through it, fleeing. He felt all his manhood evaporate at that moment. He'd lost his marbles, as Flokes liked to tell him. Tevin couldn't help Flokes.

"Grab him," Tevin heard Snarls say.

Tevin slung the chalkboard loop around his neck and ran as fast as he could muster. He heard the thumping of Dockpoint Daggers behind. They were gaining on him.

He still held the pouch of marbles in his hand and, after a moment, upended the pouch behind him. The marbles scattered across the alleyway, and the boot steps slowed as the thugs navigated the mess.

Tevin reached the rotten crates, meeting the gaze of two

confused men. Phlegm stepped forward, hand outstretched, a puzzled look crossing his face. Tevin ran straight towards him, grabbing the chalkboard and ramming it into Phlegm's stomach.

Phlegm gasped, reeling backwards, and Tevin slipped through the crates, sprinting away from Dockpoint Alley, and disappearing into the crowded streets of Bryn.

He was both nauseated and hungry; he hadn't eaten yet today. Tevin wanted to get something to eat, something that might calm his nerves, but Snarls had his money. Had his marbles, too. And Flokes. Tevin wondered if Flokes was dead. He looked around for a town guardsman, then realized he should probably write a message first.

Bendicio Flokes murdered in Dockpoint Alley. Keithan Stonebark stabbed him.

Tevin found a guard, thrusting the chalkboard into his chest. The guardsman read the message, turned to his partner. "This kid says there's been a murder in Dockpoint Alley."

"Keithan's gang finally killed somebody?"

"Seems so. All right, kid, we're going to get a regiment together. Dockpoint Alley can be a bit busy. Might need the extra help."

The guardsmen left Tevin standing there, wondering what would happen next. He didn't know what to do. He could go to the docks, find his mother and father. But the stevedores worked hard and didn't enjoy getting interrupted. Their master would be even less pleased to have a kid come running in spreading rumors of murder. Even if said murder was witnessed firsthand. The master wouldn't care.

So instead, Tevin went home. He found a half-finished loaf of bread on the kitchen counter, ripped a piece off, and ate it plain. Then he went into his room, climbed into his bed, and pulled the blanket up and over his head. He lay there, thinking, hiding. Tevin didn't feel right. Didn't feel like running had been the right option. He should've fought them. Instead, he'd lost his marbles, both the ones in his pouch and… the other ones in his other pouch. He was nothing.

He lay there until his eyes drifted closed and sleep took him. When he woke, his parents were home. After much effort, Tevin forced himself out of bed and explained to his parents what had happened. Astonished and appalled, his parents forbade him to leave the house. They also promised to find out what happened to Bendicio Flokes.

The following day, Tevin learned his best friend had died protecting him. The Bryn town guardsman had found his body discarded in another alleyway. Nothing happened to Keithan "Snarls" Stonebark. Nothing happened to the Dockpoint Daggers. Tevin didn't know if the guardsmen he'd reported the incident to ever did anything about it. He attempted two other times to report the crime, but nobody seemed to care.

One day, Tevin Whitestar promised, he'd get back at the Dockpoint Daggers. From that day forth, whenever he looked at his favorite shooting marble—the marble he'd been able to keep—he thought of Bendicio Flokes. Tevin named it Flokes, after his friend. And every time he held the marble, he felt as if his friend was with him.

Tevin would get his marbles back. Both sets.

NO RESPECT

Velturo Ondakka, one of several dukes of Anepolis—capital of Calrym—opened his eyes. He stretched, yawning, working out the kinks of sleep in his neck and back. His wife, Glendys, had already fled the bed, as she was apt to do. He didn't blame her. If he'd married himself, he'd hide as much as possible, too. Fortunately, Glendys performed her duties well—took care of the children, made sure he ate three hearty meals a day, and relieved his stress every night—if he hadn't been rich, he never would've landed her. In one way, Velturo felt bad for her. In another, he didn't—Glendys had a wonderful life, and he didn't require much.

He groaned, arched his back, stretched again. Over the top of his distended stomach, he saw the toes on his right foot curling up, silk sheet missing. He'd kicked it off again. *Too hot, much too hot.* His eyes landed upon a stain on the sheets. *Is that mustard?* Velturo sniffed the sheet, licked the stain. A faint pungent sweetness bit his tongue. "It *is* mustard."

It wasn't normal for Velturo to get food before he stumbled out of bed. Cheerful, he rolled out from beneath the sheets and slipped his feet into felt slippers. He pulled on a light robe to cover his naked body, yawned, and traipsed into the dining hall. *It should be mandatory to eat one's first meal in bed.*

At the table, Glendys sat at its head, their two children flanking her. Velturo took his spot at the foot of the table, where Glendys *should* be sitting. It'd been this way since the wedding. "Velturo, dear, if you're married to a beautiful woman like me, and I have to look at you all day, it's only fair I get to sit here," she'd said when he'd first complained. He didn't argue or care, though. Beautiful woman, delicious food, enough money to live a comfortable rest of his life.

He recalled the threat Ardus, Glendys's brother, once told him, "If you upset my sister, I will kill you." Velturo lived life afraid this would come to fruition. His wife never mentioned Ardus's threat, and he hoped she'd forgotten about the vow her brother made on her wedding day. Velturo didn't argue with Glendys because he didn't want Ardus to murder him.

"Glendys, darling, there's a mustard stain on the sheets, ah-hah." Whenever he was around anyone, even his wife, he couldn't prevent that laugh from escaping. He'd found long ago people reacted better to laughter, and so he laughed. Which turned into laughing about everything.

His wife sighed. "Are you sure it's food? Perhaps you didn't finish in the privy."

Their two sons giggled at that word. Velturo frowned. "I tasted it. It was mustard, ah-hah." He sat, listening to the groans of his children. *No respect. Nobody has any respect.*

"It could've been poo!" his oldest, Culbern, said, a look of disgust on his face.

The youngest son, Benford, stuck his tongue out, giggling and clapping his hands. "Poo! Poo!"

Velturo sighed. It reminded him of attending a council meeting at the Great Hall—a collection of people sitting around a table, poking at their food, and taking jabs at him. *No respect.* He looked at the plate sitting in front of him. A couple slices of white bread, half a fish, some sausage, and stewed carrots. He sipped the red wine a servant had already poured. "Splendid meal, ah-hah." *Hearty, filling, tasty.*

"Papa, it could've been poo," Culbern said, again.

"Do you think I'm a fool, Cully?" Velturo, irritated, picked up a fork and stabbed it into a sausage. The scraping of silver on silver and the chinking of plate reverberating off wood. He realized he hadn't laughed—a sign of genuine anger. His family picked up on it, silencing themselves.

He ate, drank wine, and shot glares across the table at his wife, who sat in *his* rightful chair. She ignored him, focused on her meal, and occasionally assisted Benford.

"I directed the staff to make lamb root pie tonight," Glendys said, out of nowhere.

He swallowed a mouthful of tender, succulent fish. Velturo smiled, then swallowed again for good measure. No sense in choking while he spoke—something which occurred more than he liked. "Nothing fixes a day like lamb root pie." It was his favorite food, and Glendys knew it. His face burned with shame. Another sip of wine, then he said, "I'm sorry, ah-hah."

"Don't be. You're a busy man, working for the king. You have two lovely children. You have an even lovelier wife. The fact these," Glendys cleared her throat, glancing at Culbern who was listening intently. She mouthed the words "pig fuckers," then continued, "are treating you in the way they—"

"Mum?"

Glendys gave a stern look at Culbern. "Don't interrupt." She turned back to Velturo. "The fact they insult and ignore you is a problem they'll one day have to overcome. You're worth more than that." He wasn't but he was grateful for the compliment.

"Mum?"

"Oh, for the love of Mother Avani, what do you want, dear child?"

"What's 'pig fuckers'?"

Glendys screeched, and Velturo thumped the table with his fist. "Quiet, you, ah-hah!" he half-shouted, half-laughed. He didn't know how to react.

Culbern's eyes widened, and he sank into his chair, realizing he'd done something wrong.

Gathering herself, Glendys explained that he'd misread her lips, and it was rude to do so.

Velturo spent the next few minutes finishing his breakfast, loathing the upcoming council meeting. He knew what was awaiting him. He'd just continue to do what he'd been training for the last few years—contribute to the discussion while eating and drinking and ignoring the bastards.

Midway through Glendys's lecture, Velturo stood, smoothing his robe and brushing crumbs to the floor. He noticed he'd dribbled wine down his front at some point. *Typical.* "I need to get ready for work, ah-hah." His wife ignored him, and Culbern was too busy learning the difference between reading lips and normal discussion, so Velturo waved to Benford—who returned the wave—and departed to find someone able to assist him in getting ready for the day.

Sarla had, as usual, prepared him as best she could. She was his favored servant and could always get clothes to fit in ways nobody else seemed capable. Although it mattered little, within an hour or two, he'd spill something on whatever he wore. And, as usual, she'd accompanied him—along with a contingent of armed guards—through the streets of Lochwall, to the council of King Mikas Garcovi and the rest of the dukes and duchesses who met there.

"Here," Velturo said, dropping several coins into Sarla's palm, "fetch yourself something to eat. And bring back a chocolate custard from the bakery, ah-hah." If lamb root pie was on the menu for later, he'd make the meal even better with one of his favorite desserts.

Sarla bowed. "Yes, Lord Ondakka."

He'd commanded her not to call him that, unless around other nobility. It wasn't his style. He smiled, then waved a hand, dismissing her.

One of the king's guards positioned outside the Great Hall opened the door for Velturo. Entering the Great Hall, Velturo made his way to his regular spot—midway up the far side of the table, facing the doors he'd just entered. A spot he enjoyed. *Don't have your back to the door.* Not since these people despised him. Duke Sturgeon sat in the chair next to Velturo's. Though most in attendance hated Sturgeon almost as much as Velturo—Sturgeon spoke slower than anyone Velturo had ever met—he couldn't dislike the old man. Perhaps it was because Sturgeon stole plenty of negative atmosphere from Velturo. The table accommodated twenty-three people, plus the king, though many of the attending dukes and duchesses remained passive and silent throughout entire meetings, only chiming in whenever important, or throwing their favor behind the person who'd paid them off.

His stomach rumbled as he lowered himself into the chair. He picked up a cloth from the table, laying it in his lap, and glanced around. Shelled nuts rested in a bowl, waiting to be cracked open. Empty placeholders for other food held his gaze. He sighed. *I've come too early.* He thought this every day, but it'd be dangerous to show up late without good reason. The king would have his head.

Everyone stood as King Mikas Garcovi entered. Velturo waited a few moments, feigned surprise at having missed the king's entrance, and lifted himself a few inches off the chair, just enough to strain his muscles before the king waved them back down.

"Are we all in attendance?" the council's chancellor asked.

Velturo didn't remember the man's name. He wasn't sure anybody did.

The king groaned, closing his eyes, and rubbing his forehead. "Can you fucking see, Chancellor?" King Garcovi clenched his jaw and opened his eyes, glaring at the chancellor with habitual hatred. The chancellor was another one of Velturo's favorites in the Great Hall.

The chancellor's mouth hung open, and he stammered to get anything of worth out.

"Precisely," the king said. "So, seeing as we are all present and accounted for..." he gestured towards the dukes and duchesses, "may we continue?"

"Of cour—"

"I wasn't asking *you*, Chancellor. I was asking our esteemed lords and ladies."

"Yes, my—"

"Chancellor, if you interrupt me one more time, I will have you hanged. Do you understand?"

"Yes, my—"

"Nod, you insufferable cockroach!"

The chancellor nodded.

Several servants entered the Great Hall, and Velturo perked up. They were carrying a variety of dishes—some covered, some not. He licked his lips in anticipation. The servants set the dishes down at regular intervals on the table, and fortunately for Velturo, the closest plate held a glazed roast, dripping with juices and a light gravy. A bowl nearby contained candied chestnuts—another one of his favorite foods.

"WELL?" the king's voice echoed throughout the Great Hall, his hands splayed out in front of him.

"We may continue, my lord."

"Of course, Your Highness."

"Nothing would please me more, King Garcovi."

"This meal looks splendid, ah-hah!" Everyone's gaze

shifted to Velturo. He cleared his throat, realized the error he made, and dipped his head in the king's direction. "My apologies, Your Highness. I am ready to proceed." He straightened and slid the roast closer, then picked up the fork and knife to carve the meat, then frowned. He'd never done this before. Stabbing the fork into the roast, he sliced a large portion and placed it in front of him. Velturo saw several people giving him strange looks, and he returned the cutlery. The roast leaned to one side now, and several jagged bits stuck out. *Not the cleanest cut, but what do they expect? Should've had a servant cut it. Or maybe one of them could've. Can't do anything right here. No respect.*

"You can't go a moment without food, eh?" A jest from King Garcovi. *An improvement over anger.*

Velturo shrugged. "I like food, ah-hah."

"I'm sure you just finished a meal before entering the Great Hall," Duke Harlem Maccaro—a cheese-gobbling hypocrite—said.

"You could not disgust me more, Velturo." This in the slow, methodical, and snarky voice of Duchess Arena Hyrel. She was always one to offer an insult, no matter the target. Velturo found it ironic, considering she favored sleeping with her servants, rather than another noble. *Disgusting, the things she allows inside her.* No doubt she thought the same about him as he shoveled roast into his mouth. Juice spurted out between his lips, dribbled down his chin, and dripped down his clean clothing. *What's life without another stain?* Velturo had started believing if something didn't stain, it wasn't worth it.

"Chancellor, are you going to begin the proceedings?" King Garcovi asked, as if he hadn't just threatened to hang the man.

The chancellor, who'd slowly backed away from the king until he'd pressed against a wall, reappeared. He clapped his hands together, smiling. A grim expression on the king's face stoppered the chancellor's smile, which morphed into a face

Velturo was all too familiar with—the clenched jaw, thin-lipped contortions, and tightened cheeks Velturo often had during a bad bout of constipation.

"I have other pressing matters to attend to if there is nothing of importance taking place here," Arena said.

Velturo ignored the next few sentences passing around the table. *Probably insults. Nothing worth paying attention to... not when I have such delicious beef. How do they get it this tender? Amazing.* Velturo chewed a mouthful of the roast, savoring the meat. Swallowing, he realized he'd made a mistake—the chunk in his throat happened to still be attached to the rest in his mouth. He coughed, choked, slapped his chest with a fist. Everyone ignored him. He gasped, choked again, spluttered, and hacked. He drove his finger into his mouth, ripped the bit on his tongue from the bit in his throat, and was able to complete a successful swallow. Slobber and a string of fat dangled from his chin. Several revolted expressions made their rounds, but otherwise, nobody gave a damn he'd almost choked to death.

When he returned his focus to the conversation, the chancellor had finished briefing them and faded into shadows again. The old man sitting next to him—Duke Sturgeon—was speaking.

"It's... apparent to me... as it should be... to everyone... in attendance..." Sturgeon paused, taking several deep breaths, and continued. He'd become so frail he couldn't get a single sentence out without pausing, which focused everyone's ire on him instead of Velturo. "That we... need to consider... ramping up... local security in... anticipation... for the increased traffic... when the markets... spring back... to life... this spri—" Sturgeon mumbled the rest of the word, furrowing his brow. Then, with renewed vigor, he said, "Season."

"Nothing ever happens in the marketplace, ah-hah," Velturo said, laughing at the suggestion of criminals running amok in Anepolis, the capital city. He'd never heard of any crime taking place—not against nobility. "Too many guards patrol. Too many people. Far too many people. In order to do something amidst that many people, they'd have no respect for the people, themselves, and, worst of all, us! Not to mention a horrible disregard for their own life, ah-hah." *And who doesn't regard their own life? When one can have all this...* Velturo shoveled another forkful of roast into his mouth, closing his eyes as the decadent slice of meat collapsed around his tongue.

Across the table, Harlem plopped a chunk of cheese into his mouth, while Arena took a long sip of wine. Neither appeared pleased with Velturo's words. This was nothing new.

"Do you attend the markets, Velturo? Because the markets rarely sell prepared food, you know. I would hazard a guess you spend much of your time a street or two over, dining at a restaurant which specializes in serving... you. I'm sure you are the only customer they would need to keep their business open," Arena said, curling her lip in disgust.

Velturo ignored her, thinking about how nice it'd be to call her out on her scandalous relationships. However, that would only start further arguing, and he wanted to eat in peace.

"Is the investment worth it? Deterring crime is, of course, a chief priority," Harlem said, straightening his posture—a sign he was becoming invested, and serious. "We need to consider other issues first."

"Such as?" King Garcovi asked.

"Simply put, Mikas," a gasp as Harlem used the king's first name, "we need to focus on external threats. Remeria is in a perfect position to invade. Recalling fielded men to patrol Lochwall is unthinkable... and if we don't recall anyone, you'd have to place new recruits meant for the border in the city. It's a waste of power. Local guards are plentiful."

The king narrowed his eyes. "We cannot allow that!" He

omitted Harlem's lack of respect. *Disgusting. What a weak king.* But Velturo didn't really think that. He knew he couldn't have done better.

"Think... about... the people... My Lords... and Ladies..." Sturgeon said.

Velturo didn't give a shit about the people. Nobody in that room did. Not even Sturgeon. Or, perhaps, *he* might've. Sturgeon was the only dying one in the room, so perhaps he'd concluded his life wasn't more important than somebody else's. It wasn't like Sturgeon had anything to live for now.

He stopped listening and shoveled the rest of the roast into his mouth, chewed it, then spooned up the excess gravy and juices and swallowed that as well. Then, Velturo slid the bowl of candied chestnuts closer, and popped several in his mouth, relishing their sweetness.

His mind left the Great Hall, slipping into delusional thoughts about how grand his life was. Pretending to believe he'd made *it*. That he'd found happiness. He was rich. He had a beautiful wife who loved him unconditionally. Two sons. *Sons, damn it!* He consumed amazing food every day. But none of it was the case. He knew the truth. He wasn't happy. Velturo had money, yes, but he wasn't rich. His wife despised him but had married him to elevate her lifestyle. She knew it; he knew it; everyone in the Great Hall knew it. He ate because it provided him comfort, unlike anything else. His sons weren't even his, he was sure of that. *But whose were they?* He wasn't sure he wanted to know.

Velturo sighed, returning to the conversation. It appeared they'd come to a vote.

"I... think... we should... help the... citizens," Sturgeon said.

"I agree," another duchess said.

"I dissent with that," a duke said. "The market is safe enough."

Harlem's back became as rigid as Velturo's father.

"Remeria is too large a threat. We must focus on protecting our borders. There have been no noticeable issues before this year. There's no reason suggesting this time will be any different." *That's the key—no noticeable issues. Nobody cared otherwise.* And they wouldn't discuss the matter if there hadn't been complaints.

Scowling at Harlem, Arena shook her head. "It is ridiculous to consider abandoning the citizens in their time of need."

Velturo disagreed with Arena often. Today, however, he sided with her. "I agree—we must protect the citizens, ah-hah." He wanted to wipe the satisfied smirk off Harlem's face. *If I had called the king by his first name, I'd already be in prison. Or dead.*

The rest of the votes tallied and concluded, making it official—they'd increase this year's guard patrols around the marketplace. Harlem appeared solemn. Velturo grinned.

The rest of the meeting passed through normal functions —requests from concerned citizens, policy proposals and updates, a discussion on foreign events, and so on. Velturo tuned most of it out, focused on the candied chestnuts. And before he knew it, the meeting concluded.

Sarla and his guards filed behind him as Velturo headed home. He noticed she'd bought the requested chocolate custard, which pleased him.

Upon entering his manor, Velturo let out a heavy sigh. Attending the Great Hall took far more effort and caused more stress than it was worth. He heard his two sons rummaging around their room, and a scolding tone coming from his wife, though he didn't make out the words. The noise stopped.

Velturo passed by and, with Sarla in tow, proceeded to the

washtub—not before dropping off the custard in the kitchens and catching a whiff of the delicious-smelling lamb root pie. Then, with Sarla's help, he stripped naked and bathed. The water, much to Velturo's annoyance, was lukewarm. "Are you fucking kidding me, ah-hah?" *No respect. People have no respect.*

"My Lord?" Sarla asked. She made a decent show of not being revolted by his naked body but he knew she was just like everyone else. The large gut which hung from his frame often turned people away.

"The water feels like it's been heated by a pair of men pissing in it, rather than fire, ah-hah."

"I'll make a complaint, my lord."

"Don't bother. Just hurry. And stop with the 'my lords', ah-hah."

"Sorry, Velturo."

Several minutes later and Velturo was being wiped down by Sarla, then helped into his favorite afternoon velvet robes. He dismissed her, then spent his requisite hour with his children—today he tried to teach them a game called Checkknight, though they still weren't able to grasp the idea. Culbern seemed rather bored with the affair, and Benford decided the pair of pawns tasted better than his dirty thumb.

Velturo's heart pulsed in excitement when the meal bell rang. He herded his sons into the dining hall, affirming to Glendys they'd washed their hands—they hadn't—and sat at the foot of the table, as usual. He glared at his wife, sitting in his spot. Already food on her plate instead of his, even though Velturo was head of the family. *No respect. Nobody has any fucking respect anymore.* But he clamped his lips closed and waited for a servant to fill his plate. No use making any unnecessary noise over the matter. He'd tried before and it caused too much chaos.

It didn't matter, anyway. Tonight was lamb root pie night. He licked his lips, staring down at the heaping mass of meat pie slathered in gravy with carrots, potatoes, turnips, and a small bit of radish. Velturo could taste it before he took a single bite. He shoved the first large bite into his mouth, sighing, and allowing his body to wilt into its comfortable slouch in the chair. "Mmph."

"Pa, are you all right?" Culbern asked.

"Yeth," Velturo said, before swallowing.

Glendys waved her knife in the air at him. "It's rude to talk with your mouth full."

"My apologies, ah-hah." Velturo didn't care.

For the next several minutes, he crammed food down his throat, ignoring his family. Not that he should pay attention. He knew they'd be talking about their day—which meant they'd either remained home or gone out and done some monotonous chore he didn't care about—or inquiring about his day, which he knew they didn't care about.

"Vel, answer your son," Glendys said, a trace of heat in her voice.

Velturo looked to Benford. He was playing with his food, instead of eating it. *You could put the world's best food in front of him, and he still won't eat. No respect.* He turned to Culbern, who stared at him. Waiting. "What did you say, ah-hah?"

"Papa, I wanted to know how things went with the mean one."

Velturo glanced at his wife, who just nodded, expecting him to answer.

"The woman who sits across from you, Papa." *Duchess Arena Hyrel. Why is he bringing her up?*

"Everything went well, Cully. We even voted together on some policy. Now eat your food before it gets cold, ah-hah."

Culbern took a bite, then furrowed his brow. This could only mean one thing—another question. "But Papa, she hates you. Why would you help her?"

Velturo grumbled a curse or two.

"Answer your son."

"Sometimes you need to work with people you don't like.

It's like Checkknight… which, if you'd ever learn to play, would give you a better understanding of politics and strategy, ah-hah."

"Checkknight is boring, Papa."

"You're boring!" Velturo said, slamming his fist on the table. *No respect! Nobody had any respect.* Even if he thought Checkknight was boring, too, he wanted to teach his sons the art.

"Velturo Ondakka, what's the matter with you?" Glendys stood, lips curled back and her teeth bared like a rabid dog. He heard his sons crying.

"I'm full." He wasn't. "It's time for bed." He'd lay in bed staring at the ceiling. "Good night, ah-hah."

"You're leaving? You haven't even had dessert!"

Velturo never left without dessert. "I won't tolerate the lack of respect anymore, ah-hah!" And stormed out.

He laid in bed, staring at the ceiling, stomach rumbling. His wife came to bed late. As he knew she would. She tried to talk to him and he pretended to sleep, even though he knew she knew he wasn't asleep. It happened as he knew it would. Once Velturo was sure she was dreaming, he snuck out, ate his fill of lamb root pie, and a heaping serving of chocolate custard. He thought about Ardus. "If you upset my sister, I will kill you," he'd said. Velturo believed it. He'd need to fix things tomorrow night. He'd take the day to clear his mind, and hoped she'd do the same.

The next day, he woke, skipped breakfast, and stormed out of the house without an escort. Upon reflection, he'd realized this should've meant something.

Velturo went to a local restaurant, ate a meal, attended the meeting at the Great Hall… except there wasn't one. He'd apparently missed the part during the previous meeting when King Garcovi had cancelled today's counsel. Nothing unusual. Velturo had just missed it—which explained why his guards hadn't met him. *I must've been busy eating.* He didn't want to go home, so he milled about the city, realizing how nice it was to be alone. No wife, no children, no escort. Although the occasional glance from people of meager wealth unnerved him, he otherwise enjoyed not having a servant doting on him, or a guard steering him in various directions.

At midday, Velturo went home. It'd be earlier than usual, but perhaps he'd be able to fix things with Glendys. This wasn't the first time they'd argued, nor would it be the last. He didn't want the issue to linger between them.

His house was quieter than normal when he returned home. Peeking into his sons' room, he found them both asleep. He didn't know they still slept during the day, but then again, he avoided them most of the time. Servants and his wife took care of them, as it should be. His father had once told him there was a reason his relationship with Velturo frayed over the years. "It's not a family that makes a man," he'd said, "it's what he can provide for his family. A man with a family he can't take care of is no man. If he won't take care of his family, he won't bother with himself. And a man who doesn't care about himself isn't reliable. Remember this when you become a father and your children complain about your absence." Velturo hadn't understood the advice at the time, but it made sense now. And it was a great excuse to get out of the house.

He heard what sounded like a gasp, then a scream coming from his wife. Velturo hurried towards the sound, finding himself in the hall outside his bedroom. Glendys was within, making guttural, breathy noises. Pleasured noises he'd never heard. The door to the room wasn't completely latched, so he edged it open. Velturo peeked inside and his eyes met a frightening sight—his wife, legs spread in a "v" and up in the air, a hairy and thin man on top of her, giving Glendys the hammer and nail treatment. Velturo gasped, pulling back from the doorway. There wasn't a moment in his marriage Velturo had any delusions of grandeur. They weren't the perfect family. She'd married him for a better life. He'd married her because he couldn't find any other prospects and she was prettier than most. *No respect. No fucking respect. Nobody treats me right!* And it was true. Nobody treated him right. But what could he do about that? Nothing.

Instead of raising a fuss over the matter—no doubt she was acting out in spite of their previous argument—he stifled his anger and retrieved a significant portion of chocolate custard from the kitchen. *Something to ease the mind.* He sat at the head of the table, pleased with the rebellious act. *Perhaps things could be different now. Perhaps I'll take charge. My father would kill me if he saw how I was treated.* "You've become a nursemaid," his father would've said. And he had. Without the nursing. Or the maid. He was ordered around like one, however.

He finished his custard and remained in the chair, waiting for Glendys to catch him in the act. When Glendys appeared, however, she took him off guard, because next to her, red and sweaty, stood her brother, Ardus.

"Velturo, you're home," Glendys said, surprised.

He took a moment to clear his mind, realizing his wife was fucking her brother. His *wife* was fucking her *brother. Disgusting!*

"You're fucking each other, ah-hah?"

They glanced at each other. *These are the parents of my sons? A brother and sister?* He felt sickened.

"If you tell anyone, I will kill you," Ardus said. Velturo believed him.

"I want my chair back, ah-hah." It was the only request he had.

"Fine," Glendys said. "Twice a week Ardus comes here."

Velturo wanted to retch. *No respect.* But life was politics, and there wasn't respect within politics. He ground his teeth together. "Fine, ah-hah." That damned laugh. It'd never make him sound fearsome.

It wasn't worth fighting over. He would've had to get divorced, which would cripple his tenuous position in Lochwall. He'd become more of a laughing-stock than he already was. Velturo had his chair back. Starting today, he'd work to become the man his father assumed he would be. Even if the road meant he'd get no respect from anyone. *No respect,* he thought. *Nobody has any fucking respect for me.*

And they didn't. But he lived with that knowledge just fine.

A TALE OF TWO TWINS

Vellory Dormante and Corkel "Corky" Rebbins were twins. Or, at least, they called themselves twins. Because of their strange and miraculous situation, it felt right. They were both born twins. Vellory's brother, Ernault, died of pneumonia a year and a half after they'd been born. Corky's brother, Sorkel, died when they were three years old. Nobody ever identified why—some people just weren't meant to live. Vellory and Corky were also the same age and had attended school together. And, for being unrelated, they looked remarkably similar, although some of this was, admittedly, fabricated by themselves.

They both had short brown hair—though Vellory's was a shade darker than Corky's—and brown eyes. They were both tanned from all the time they spent outside. And the pair often matched their clothing.

Vellory was four cycles older than Corky, and Corky was two decades smarter than Vellory. She could admit that. Vellory, however, could lift two heavy bricks, while Corky was lucky if he could lift two large stones. Vellory was half a foot taller than Corky, and much thicker, as well. They complemented one another, fitting like the twins they'd lost. They'd become each other's replacement twins.

They had both been born in the capital of Remeria, Andora. And even though Remeria's king lived here, even though the city was richer beyond imagination, secured by leagues of soldiers and Magicai alike, there was, of course, a squalor. Squalor in which Vellory and Corky had become familiar. Neither of the Dormante or Rebbins families were starving, but they hadn't ever thrived, either. With every one of age occupied by work, Vellory and her brother ended up entertaining themselves—and did what they could to help provide. And now, with Corky's developing secret, that had become both easier and more difficult than ever before.

She didn't understand what was happening. Vellory struggled with thinking about anything she didn't experience herself, and she was fine admitting that. Somehow, in some way, Corky had developed powers. Powers the Magicai had. Powers Corky *shouldn't* have. Not without the proper training and schooling. She remembered when he'd tried to explain to her what he thought had happened. "I don't know what happened, Vel. Somehow, something just… *popped*, I guess. Something inside me. And now I can do things."

Vellory hadn't believed him at first. They'd played pretend many times over and she'd thought it was another of those instances, in which Corky was a Magicus, and Vellory played his noble guardsman, a Remerian knight. A laughable role for Vellory to play, as Remerian women didn't serve as soldiers. The Falcon Knights in the north, in the country of Cyrok, allowed women to become knights. But something about pretending to be another country's warrior didn't rest well with her, either. So she'd remained a Remerian knight. Loyal to the crown, she was. Always. When Corky had showed her how he could conjure fire in the palm of his hand, she hadn't believed him still. "A mere parlor trick," she said, in her best imitation of nobility.

He, of course, hadn't been lying. And when he'd conjured fire on a nearby pile of refuse, her eyes had near bulged out of her head. Corky hadn't been roleplaying or fibbing after all. And when he put the fire out by pulling it back into the alleyway's stone walkway, she'd realized just how powerful he'd become. *Little Corky, all grown up*, she'd thought, with a big stupid grin on her face.

Vellory leaned against the paint-chipped wall of the Rebbins' house, a thick stick held in her two meaty hands. Now that Corky had powers, she wondered if it was even necessary, but she figured not everything could be magicked away with the flick of a few fingers, and so she'd remain prepared. *And I'm not always with Corky*, she rationalized. On the streets, you never could be sure who you'd encounter. Vagrants, thieves, bullies, and other ne'er-do-wells, none of which she wanted to deal with without her trusty Bonebreaker—an as-of-yet unproven name she'd given to the club.

Bonebreaker thumped against the wall of the Rebbins' house. She knocked it gently—didn't want to put a hole in the plaster—but loud enough for Corky to hear. "Could you take any longer?" she asked, loud enough for him to hear.

"I'm coming!" his voice said through the window, muffled by what sounded like clothing.

Good. He's changed. Maybe he'll be done soon. She sighed, tapping Bonebreaker against her boot, staring at the early dawning sky.

The door to the Rebbins' house opened, then shut. Corky, short, thin, and fragile, walked with an awkward gait and stood in front of her, posed with his hands on his hips and a wide, beaming grin on his face. "Sorry, Vel, I—"

"You overslept again, yeah, yeah, I know that." The damn boy had been oversleeping every day for the past half cycle. She was beginning to wonder if he'd ever achieve enough sleep to satisfy his new requirements.

Corky shrugged. "Yeah, well, I'm—" He paused to yawn,

closing his eyes and stretching his arms, his yellowed teeth reflecting the sun's glow. "I'm just tired. I hope it's not a side effect of, well, you know."

"Nah," Vellory said. "I overheard my mum talking to our neighbor, Heletta, who has a growing son herself. Says he sleeps constantly, but that's normal. 'Growing boys take years to catch up to growing women', she said." Vellory smirked, nudging Corky with Bonebreaker. "Seems she's right, Puny."

Corky's eyes narrowed. "Don't call me that. You know I could burn you alive."

Vellory smiled, but inside, her heart turned to ice. She knew he was speaking the truth, but she didn't want him to see her fear. Didn't want him to have that power over her. "Right, well, let's go."

They were late, but she figured it wouldn't matter. Vellory's parents worked on Judge Lucard's pair of ferries, which ran up and down the river, bringing fresh produce to Andora from Rivane and Maceport. Vellory knew little about the business, but she knew it was hard labor, and she knew Judge Lucard was always looking for extra—and cheap—hands. And, while Vellory's parents were off in Maceport, unloading one of Judge's ferries, Vellory and Corky, with no parental permission, had signed up for the other ferry, which was due to leave for Rivane later that day.

The twins had decided it was time to make money. All working hands needed to contribute to their families when living in the slums, and if twelve-year-old Millich Garlo could work with his blacksmithing father, then Vellory and Corky could unload a few crates and barrels, she'd figured. Corky had agreed, so they'd inquired with Judge's secretary, a sharp-nosed cranky woman who'd agreed to give them work, provided they took a quarter of what an adult man would be paid and did a complete day's work. The secretary framed this as "learning" and "you should be grateful for any opportunity which comes *your* way," the secretary had said, as if they were scum being given a chance. Which, in Vellory's mind, the crotchety old woman probably *was* thinking in her head. It was a good thing Vellory hadn't been holding Bone-breaker at that moment in time, having left it on the bench out front at Corky's request.

They weaved their way through the cracked and faded cobblestone streets of the slums, making their way to the gate on the eastern side of the city, where Judge Lucard and his men would be preparing the ferry. Once the twins had exited through the gate—a guardsman giving them a suspicious glance, followed by a hesitant nod—they made their way over to the ferry. Stenciled on the side of the large boat was the ferry's name, *Lucky Lucard*. Vellory's parents must've taken the *Judge Fairly*.

"Stupid name," Vellory said, not for the first time.

"Shut up, Vel. Don't let anyone hear that talk. We'll be kicked off the boat before we ever step foot on it."

"Right, I know, I know. I'll watch my tongue."

"Watch your face, too, because you got that stupid grin. Makes people think you're laughing at them."

He was right, she knew. She fixed her face.

A tall, burly man, with a thick black beard flecked with bits of gray, and a balding pate, hollered out orders. He wiped his shining head with a stained kerchief, wiped his face with it. Probably mopped every part of his body with that disgusting rag, she figured—all of which was drenched in the most pungent sweat she'd ever smelled.

He noticed the twins approaching, and snorted a glob from his throat, hacking it into the grass he stood in. "Yer late." Vellory knew the man. He was Judge's second-in-command, his First Mate, Gillings Kovac.

"Aye," she said. "He overslept." She threw her thumb in Corky's direction.

"I don't give no fucks," Gillings said. "Get over there," he pointed at a stack of crates and a cluster of barrels, "and start moving that pile on there." He swiveled his finger to the *Lucky Lucard.* "We don't allow no slackin', no we don't. You slack anymore, I'll kick ye off the boat while on the river, don't doubt that. Don't doubt that at all. Now get down there and see if you even have the strength to move anything." Gillings shook his head, upset, then muttered to himself but loud enough the twins could hear, "Fucking kids. Why do you do this to me, Judge?" He wiped his forehead again and another whiff of pungent armpit reached her nose.

"Come on," Corky said, pulling on Vellory's shirt.

She followed him, realizing Corky had pulled her away from staring at Gillings in revulsion.

"He reeks!"

"Come *on!*" Corky said, yanking her toward the stack of unloaded crates. When they were further away from the First Mate, Corky glared at her and then proceeded to reprimand her. "You can't say things like that, Vel. He could have heard you. That's Judge Lucard's second. What do you think he would've done if he heard you? We wouldn't have *any* work. Your parents might've lost their jobs!"

"A blessing from Mother Avani, if I've ever heard one," she said. "Maybe they could find work that pays decent wages."

"Remember why we're here, Vel. We need to provide money for our family. Not ruin our parents' lives."

"I got it," Vellory said. She realized her hands hurt and loosened their tightened grip on Bonebreaker. She needed to keep her anger in check. Corky was right. They were here to help their families, not create more hardships.

They reached the closest stack of crates, and Vellory realized how much more difficult this was going to be than she'd originally thought. She figured she might lift a crate, but Corky would be too small.

"Hey!"

The twins turned their gaze to a man who'd clearly tried

to clean himself up, but failed. His beard was trimmed, but uneven. He'd soaked his hair in so much oil it was almost dripping and it stuck out in stiff spikes, pointing in various directions. A scent of a very feminine mixture of both lavender and chamomile reached her nose. Vellory wondered why everything seemed to stink today.

The man had jogged over to the twins. "Are you the new loaders?"

"Don't you mean 'dockhand'?'" Corky asked.

"That?" Flummoxed, the man gestured at the small dock leading to the *Lucky Lucard*. "I don't consider that a dock. So you're loaders. Work on a real ship, on a real dock, and I'll call you a dockhand. Here, you're working on a ferry. Why are you even asking? You a priest or something?"

"Just a boy with a mouth too large for his body," Vellory said.

"Aye. If you want to leave anything on the *Lucky*, go ahead, but be quick. There's an open crate you can store your stuff in. Then get back here and start shifting cargo. I'm the master loader here, so you'll report to me. My name's Pasco, but you'll call me 'sir'."

"I'm Corky, that's Vellory."

"I didn't ask. Now get your shit on the *Lucky* and start working, or you'll earn nothing, eh? And don't forget the 'sir', or I'll tell Judge you're useless." Pasco shook his head in disgust, his spiked hair wobbling. He looked a fool, and Vellory had to restrain a laugh.

The twins dodged several loaders, crossing the narrow dock, walking up a plank, and then were aboard the *Lucky Lucard*.

Vellory spotted a large, lidless crate among the lidded ones. Approaching it, she peered inside and saw various possessions. Bags, articles of clothing, a bottle of rum. Vellory laid Bonebreaker inside the crate, careful to avoid shattering the bottle. If there was one thing she'd learned from her parents, it was that these men took alcohol more seriously than their own families. Her parents had told her countless stories of drunken coworkers where she knew enough to not play with fate.

She glanced at Corky and he shrugged, as he had nothing to deposit.

"Well, off to work, then?" Vellory asked. "Although I'm not sure how you're going to manage."

Corky snorted. "I'll figure something out." He had a suspicious look about him, like he was hiding something.

She suspected it meant something to do with his newfound powers. She hoped Pasco didn't notice. Vellory didn't want him to think they were cheating. Or they harbored a curse. People who worked on water believed in lots of superstitions, she'd learned. Her parents had told her plenty of tales about that, too.

They disembarked the ferry after waiting for a pair of loaders hauling crates to pass, then returned to the cargo. Pasco had already disappeared, though Vellory assumed he was somewhere nearby, monitoring them. She knew how important it was, when on water, that a crew trusts one another. Even if that water was just a river.

"Now, then," Corky said, examining the crates. "I suppose I'll just grab one."

Vellory crossed her arms and waited, eyebrow raised, for Corky to lift a crate himself.

He caught her staring at him. "What?"

"You couldn't lift a crate half that size."

"Not before," he said. Corky held a hand up and the crate *floated* off the stack. He walked towards the *Lucky*, the crate hovering in front of him.

Vellory's jaw dropped.

"Well, grab a crate then, Vel," he said. Corky shifted his hands to either side of the crate, making it appear as if he was carrying it.

She slid one off the stack, and her arms dropped from the weight. She had to use more muscle than she'd expected. Dirt fell from the cracks of the crate, and a horrible odor reached her nose. "What in the name of Mother Avani are they packing in these?"

Vellory caught a whiff of pungent sweat and she knew First Mate Gillings was behind her. *Everything is just going to smell terrible today.*

"If you wondered less and spent more time working, the *Lucky* would be loaded already," he said. "Hurry up, you're walking too slow. You need to earn the money you'll be paid, or you won't see any of it—we needed this shit packed an hour ago, if we're to make the deadline Judge set for us." A fraction of a moment passed and then he said, "I said double time it, kids!"

The twins hurried forward, passing a group of loaders returning for their next load. After two more trips, Vellory began panting. The strain on her thighs and forearms and shoulders and back was making her ache everywhere. For her age, Vellory was very strong. Compared to Corky, she was a lioness compared to a kitten. But, when compared to the other grown men loading the *Lucky*, she was nothing—a kitten to a lion, she figured. Meanwhile, Corky wasn't exhausted at all.

As the sun climbed higher, sweat covered more and more of her body. She wondered if she'd start smelling like First Mate Gillings. A glance at her blackened hands told her she'd at least stink of whatever was inside the crates.

It took about two hours for the *Lucky* to be fully loaded, Vellory guessed. And by then, she'd become thoroughly exhausted, but she'd somehow kept up with the pace of the other loaders. Corky grinned at her, not even perspiring a little. The sailors kept tossing nervous glances in Corky's direction. *They probably suspect he's possessed or something.*

The master loader, Pasco—who Vellory hadn't seen load a single crate or barrel—reappeared when the work was done.

"Good, you loaded and you kept a decent pace. First Mate Gillings says you're allowed to stay on. Judge'll be accompanying us on this one—he has business in Rivane. So." Pasco paused, scratching his stiff, over-oiled hair. "Mind your orders and keep out of the way of the officers. Now, get aboard the ferry. We leave as soon as Judge arrives."

The twins boarded the *Lucky Lucard*—after rinsing their hands in the river—and found an open crate of semi-ripe apples sitting on the deck. Loaders were dishing them out to everyone who'd helped, and Vellory and Corky were each given a pair. They made their way to the rear of the ferry— Vellory retrieved Bonebreaker, just in case—escaping most of the loud men who were talking about the trip ahead or reminiscing about previous trips or boasting about various feats accomplished or wild tales experienced while on actual ships sailing in saltwater.

Vellory noticed the black dirt still stuck to her skin. She wiped her hands off—and the apples she'd touched—as well as she could, before sinking her teeth in. Flecks of juice squirted out and peppered her cheek. She wiped the juice off with a hand, grinning as she chewed. Fresh apples. They weren't the ripest, nor the sweetest, but they were still a treat she'd not had in some time. They ate their apples, watching the river flow past and engaging in small talk.

During their conversation, her eyes met Corky's, and she wondered what seemed different about him. She couldn't place it, but something… had changed. He looked older. Wiser, maybe. His babied face had lost some of its youth. He looked more like his age, and earlier, just before they'd started loading, she hadn't noticed it. She needed to pay more attention.

The silence aboard the ferry eroded the rest of her thoughts. She and Corky both craned their necks, trying to see what was happening. There were too many loaders in the way, though. They made their way closer to the crowd and saw what'd happened—Judge Lucard had boarded.

Commanding the attention and standing in the center of the loaders—flanked by both Gillings and Pasco—was a short, squat, bald man with a patchy beard and a jagged scar crossing his forehead addressed everyone. Judge Lucard. Vellory recognized him from her parent's description.

"This trip is a little different," Judge said, waving his arms like he was a troupe performer or an important philosopher. "A business partner of mine has signed a contract granting my ferries, *Lucky Lucard* and *Judge Fairly,* exclusivity in Rivane's citrus fruits. He's the largest citrus fruit farmer in Rivane, and his competition has been trickling out of business. Nobody can compete with his quality, however much they try. However, he doesn't want money. You may have noticed the cargo is more than usual this trip. That's because Fenland's Farms has expanded tenfold over the last few years. They need more fertilizer. And the cattle that exist in Rivane aren't providing enough—and it's divvied up amongst the other farmers. A deal was struck. In return for exclusivity, I've agreed to bring as much fertilizer as we can safely transport, without losing our other business."

Vellory glanced at her dirtied hands, disgusted that she'd just eaten apples stained with shit. She recalled Gillings' words from earlier, "we needed this shit packed an hour ago." She wondered if that had been coincidence or a joke.

Judge took a moment to take a sip from a canteen that hung at his hip. Then, nonchalantly, he added, "Who knew a city's sewers could be so lucrative?"

It took a moment before what he'd said processed with Vellory. Corky was already retching. She looked back at her palms and bile rose in her throat.

Outraged loaders gagged while others laughed.

The cacophony of retching and gagging and vomiting was too much for Vellory and she leaned over the side of the

Lucky, spewing chunks of apple and a brown liquid—remnants of her porridge breakfast, no doubt. Her throat burned from the acid, and she searched for water. Several other loaders had popped open a barrel and were dipping gourds into it, pouring water into their mouths. Vellory joined them and, after getting a drink herself, she rejoined Corky, who'd been able to keep his stomach in check.

Judge, Gillings, and Pasco chuckled.

Corky was shaking his head. "Gross," he said. "Just gross."

"All right," Judge said. "Let's set sail."

The loaders cheered. A few moments later, the *Lucky Lucard* pulled away from the makeshift dock and they were traveling upriver toward Rivane. The loaders seemed to double as deckhands, she realized, and most of them picked up various tasks. Some were setting up a canopy to block the sun, while others were poling the ferry. It appeared everyone had accepted the cargo without issue, but Vellory was still disgusted, and judging by Corky's expression, he was as well.

Vellory opened her mouth to talk, but Corky cut her off. "Vel," he said, nodding behind her.

She turned, and Judge was a mere foot away, beaming at her. "You're the Dormante's child, yes? Mel?"

"Vel. Vellory. Yes, sir," she said. She wanted to sound strong, confident, but his sudden and unexpected appearance created a stammer she wasn't used to having. Judge was her parents' employer. She didn't want to disappoint him or cause any problems. Her parents would never forgive her.

"Vel, yes, yes, of course. My apologies." His smile widened in to a great beaming arch, filled with perfectly shined, white teeth. "And this is your friend? The other child we've taken on?"

"Corkel Rebbins, sir," he said.

"Right. I'm unfamiliar with your family name," Judge said, maintaining his smile, but Vellory swore she saw a finite shift in expression—one of disdain. Anyone Judge wasn't aware of wasn't important to him, she realized.

"My father works in the stables, my mother works as a baker's assistant."

"Ah," Judge said, nodding, though his smile had shifted into a grimace. "I see." He shifted his attention back to Vellory. "Well!" Then he clapped his hands and his jovial expression returned. "Now we're off to Rivane, with nothing but the comfortable swells of a gentle river and the friendly comradeship of other like-minded folks, eh?"

Vellory nodded, and Judge returned the nod.

"Very good," he said. "Well, good work so far. Listen to Gillings and Pasco, and we'll be fine."

"Yes, Captain!" Corky said.

Judge snorted. "Captain? Don't tell me they started with these ship terms again. I'll have Gillings and Pasco both flayed." He shook his head in what seemed to Vellory to be genuine annoyance. "Imbeciles. Gillings *is* my second, and Pasco *is* the best loader I have, but they are neither first mate nor master loader, and although they should be received with proper respect, you don't have to treat them like ship officers." And with that, Judge spat over the side of the *Lucky* and stormed off toward Gillings and Pasco.

"Oh, well, that's good, Corky. I don't know how to act properly on a ship. Glad we aren't pretending to be on one anymore. I know what my parents have said, but neither of them have been aboard a proper ship, either."

"I wouldn't take his words too much to heart, Vel. I doubt Gillings or Pasco will be as happy to hear their names without the titles they repudiate."

Vellory frowned. "Repudiate?"

"Yeah. It means to really like something, I think."

"What?"

"I overheard somebody use it the other day, Vel. I'm just trying to expand my versatility with language."

"Well, I don't repudiate that idea."

"That's now how the word works," Corky said, sighing.

A voice calling from across the ferry interrupted their argument. "Hey, kids! Get over here and learn how to pole a ferry, yeah? We aren't paying you to stand there looking pretty!"

Vellory saw it was Gillings, waving them over. "Gross," she said, dreading his odor.

"Well, let's get to it, I guess," Corky said.

The twins learned to pole the ship, which turned out to be more laborious than it looked. Corky's arms couldn't handle more than a few minutes of the exercise, so he'd resorted to using his powers to assist. With every stroke, he'd funnel his power into the wood and it'd achieve the power of more than a grown man poling. He explained this to Vellory as they took turns on a pole, changing out in hour-long shifts. Vellory's hands ached. They were raw and she could feel callouses forming. Corky's remained just as soft and unworked as ever, but he'd started sprouting facial hair.

Vellory was no expert, but she found that odd. He'd not had any earlier and now he had several whiskers protruding from both his chin and upper lip. When she'd noticed, he'd proudly searched them out with his fingers and tongue. After he'd discovered them, he hadn't stopped talking about it.

Between the poling and discussion about hair, Vellory was ready for a change of activity. But change didn't come. They took turns poling all afternoon. When the sunlight had almost disappeared, Gillings called a halt. They anchored the ferry close to shore, and on the bank of the river created a pair of fires to both cook on and provide light. On the *Lucky*, Judge had lit several lanterns, hanging them from hooks on the canvas the loaders had raised earlier.

Vellory and Corky took the opportunity to wash their hands thoroughly in the water. Judge even provided a bar of soap for the loaders to bathe if they wished, and Vellory and Corky scrubbed their hands raw.

They ate a filling meal of salted beef pottage, and bedrolls were laid out on the *Lucky*. A watch was kept all night long, and the twins each took a turn during different shifts. During Vellory's shift, her companion, who'd had a whispered conversation with her during their three-hour shift, explained there was always a chance of being raided and, although unlikely, some ferries had reportedly been robbed of everything they'd been transporting. One ferry, he told her, had lost its entire crew to one of these raids.

The following day, Vellory notice something off about Corky. The twins spent the morning poling. When they finished, Corky had changed again.

"Something strange is happening. You've grown taller. And you have more hair on your face. This isn't natural," she said.

"Well, I am a growing boy. And growing boys grow fast, my mother always says," Corky said.

Vellory shook her head. "No, it's not right. Boys don't grow hair that fast, nor do they wake up one day and find themselves a whole inch taller than the day before. It's gotta be your powers. Something is changing you."

"You're too suspicious, Vel. You need to stop listening to the fables your parents tell you."

She wondered if he was right. Her parents had told her many tales. She considered she'd maybe inherited a sailor's suspicions and become paranoid about being on a boat, on water. Vellory shook her head. "No. I don't think so. It's not right to change so quickly. Something's not right."

"It's not my powers, Vel. I've used them before and been fine."

"You didn't use them *this* much though, Corky."

"I'm fine, Vellory," he said, and that ended it.

She wouldn't argue with him when he'd used her full name. She'd learned long ago when he was that firm, it'd just end in a shouting match and neither of them would concede defeat. Vellory didn't want that.

"Kids!" Gillings called.

She traded an annoyed glance with Corky. By now, Gillings should know their names. She figured he did and was just degrading them in front of the other men.

She retrieved Bonebreaker from where she'd set it—she carried it everywhere on the ferry—and they walked over to Gillings. He stood in front of several barrels. "These barrels are full of ripening fruit," he said. Vellory tried to stop her breathing as she closed the distance to the smelly man. "This barrel," he kicked one of them, "is empty. These barrels," his hand tapped the tops of three others, "are full. Your duty is to sort through all this fruit. Find any rotten or unusable prod-ucts, and toss them in here." He kicked the empty barrel with his boot. "These are a gift for Fenland's Farms, and Judge wants to only deliver the best of the best, to show we also understand what quality fruit is. Understood?"

The twins nodded.

"I said, 'understood'?"

"Yes, sir," the twins both said in unison.

"Good. Be quick about it. Judge wants it done in a few hours." Gillings thumped his fist off the side of the empty barrel before leaving them to their work.

"Great," Vellory said. "This is going to take forever. I doubt Judge wants it done so fast."

"We'll do it quicker," Corky said, grinning.

"How? There are—" Vellory paused. "You're talking about using more power."

"Yes."

"Don't, Corky. I don't think it's a good idea."

"If Magicai around the world can do it, I can, too."

She snorted. "Don't you think they'd be a lot more common if they could use unlimited power? We've never even *seen* a Magicus, Corky. We don't know what this does to them."

"That's because they charge lots of money, Vel. We don't live where there's money. Nobody can afford a Magicus. I bet the wealthier families *each* hire a personal Magicus to do whatever they want."

"I don't like this," she said.

Corky shrugged, then he held his hands up and the covers to each of the three barrels levitated. He shifted them to the deck of the *Lucky* and peered into the openings. "We have a barrel of grapes, a barrel of plums, and a barrel of turnips—not a fruit," he said, laughing. "Gillings is a fool."

"It doesn't matter. We still need to sort them."

Corky waved his hand and all the grapes rose into the air. "Pluck any of the bad ones out, Vel," he said. Corky was already using his power to fling the bad grapes he spotted into the empty barrel, while gently floating the good grapes back into their original barrel.

She followed suit, picking out any of the unripe, overly ripe, or rotten ones out of the air, and tossing them into the empty barrel.

A few minutes later, and Corky had finished. Vellory hadn't contributed much, she had to admit. Then she noticed the stares. Every person aboard the ferry was watching them.

"Cursed! We're cursed!" Pasco screamed. "Get them off the ship!" Several of the men crept toward the twins, seeming unsure of what to do.

Vellory reached down and grabbed Bonebreaker, just in case.

"Throw them in the water!" Pasco said, arms flailing wildly as he gestured towards the twins.

The men snapped to it and began creeping towards them. Vellory's grip tightened on Bonebreaker.

"We're not cursed!" It was Judge. "The kid's just a—"

Chaos. Half a dozen arrows peppered the advancing men, and three of them went down, injured or dead. Vellory couldn't tell. Before anything else happened, another volley of arrows took down several more men.

Then shouts from everywhere.

"Take cover!"

"We're under attack!"

"Raiders!"

"Pole to the other side of the river!" Gillings shouted out, but it was useless. One man reached for a pole, and an arrow caught him in the gut. As he clutched the wound, a second arrow slammed into his neck. He toppled over the side of the ferry, splashing into the water.

Everyone else ducked behind crates and barrels.

Vellory and Corky crouched behind the fruit barrels Gillings had tasked them to sort.

"What's happening?" Vellory asked.

"I think we're being raided," Corky said. "Don't worry," he turned to look at her, offering a reassuring smile. "I'll protect you."

It was the first time he'd ever said that and, at any other time, she'd have laughed. But she trusted him. He'd mastered his powers, and now, she believed, he could do anything he wanted.

The *Lucky* lurched in the water. She heard several loud splashes and assumed anchors had been thrown into the water. *Or people*, she considered.

She heard a crash and then the sound of boots on wood. Vellory peered over the top of the barrels and saw men in tattered clothing or worn leathers running up a makeshift gangplank, rusted swords and daggers in their hands, kerchiefs wrapped around their faces. In everyone's distraction, nobody had been pulling the ferry and it had drifted towards land. Close enough for the raiders to attack. *They must've been following us.*

Corky leaped from his position and ran towards the intruders, hand held out in front of him like a weapon. "Get off this boat!"

One invader laughed, throwing a knife at him. Corky projected a shimmering substance in front of him and the blade halted in mid-air, clattering to the ferry's deck. Then Corky laughed. He laughed in a way Vellory hadn't heard before, but she didn't like it. It sounded maniacal.

A line of flame sprayed the knife-thrower in the face and he screamed as Corky torched him. The raider's hair lit afire and he twisted and writhed as the flames raced down his clothing. Corky sprayed on until the man's screams stopped. Then he turned the flame to the next man in line, who was just jumping off the gangplank, onto the *Lucky.*

Vellory watched in both astonishment and horror as Corky burned the second man alive. A thrill of victory twittered in her heart. She grinned. *Lousy bandits trying to take what's not theirs.* She stood, Bonebreaker in her hands, and looked out on the bank. Dozens of raiders had approached the ferry, intent on boarding the boat. Now, with Corky roasting some of their comrades, they were hesitating.

The *Lucky's* crew, their hatred of Corky forgotten, had begun cheering.

With the second raider charred, his smoking body lying on the *Lucky's* deck, Corky lowered his hand, the flame disappearing.

The raiders took this as a sign to attack. They flooded forward, some crossing the gangplank, others surging through the river, to climb the ferry's side.

The *Lucky's* crew had their own weapons, cheap short swords and spears and no armor. Judge hadn't expected to be attacked, despite the risk of such an occurrence.

And then Vellory didn't have time to think. A raider with

a sword had found his way to her. She hefted Bonebreaker in her hands, suddenly petrified. She'd never had a sword fight with anyone. Vellory had pretend fights a couple times in her life, when she and Corky had imagined themselves as soldiers, but she didn't trust in her ability to defeat a grown man who intended to kill her—and Corky hadn't been the best opponent to test one's skill against.

The raider brought his sword down. Vellory saw in his expression he didn't expect resistance. He was almost correct. She gasped, realizing she needed to do something, and brought Bonebreaker up, holding each end of the club in her hands. The sword chopped into Bonebreaker. The force of the blow caused Vellory to stumble and lose her grip. She dropped Bonebreaker.

The raider kept his grip on his sword, but the weight of the club dropped and, like a pendulum, swung into the raider's thighs. He grunted as Bonebreaker smacked him, then shook his sword, trying to dislodge it from the wood. It wouldn't release.

Vellory glanced around, found nothing that could double as a makeshift weapon.

The raider dropped the sword and Bonebreaker, drawing a knife from his belt. An evil grin wormed its way across his lips and shifted into a sneer of contempt for her. "Upon second glance, you're not as young as I thought," he said. "Once me and my friends are done carving everyone else up, I will find you."

A long, jagged stone split the raider's head in half, and he crumpled to the ground.

Vellory turned and saw Corky holding his hand out toward the raider. He nodded, and she saw he'd now sported a full beard. He returned to blasting the other raiders, chipping collateral pieces of the *Lucky* off.

She returned to Bonebreaker and tried to pry the sword

out. Couldn't. She left it where it lay, picking up the knife the raider had died clutching.

Vellory left the fruit barrels and joined a majority of the *Lucky's* crew, who were gathered around Judge, Gillings, and Pasco. Everyone had fear written in their eyes. None of them, as far as Vellory could tell, had seen regular combat, for they were just as scared as she was. It wasn't until one of them spoke she realized she'd been wrong about what they were afraid of.

"He's a monster."

"Let him kill them, then we'll figure out what to do about him."

"Mother Avani save us."

She knew they had to be referring to Corky, but Vellory ignored the fools and found her way to Judge. The sound of metal on metal pierced her ears, and she realized the outer perimeter of the crew had engaged raiders who'd avoided Corky.

Judge met her eyes. "Your friend is a creating quite a stir." He rubbed his patchy beard with a hand, his eyes not quite meeting hers. He was monitoring the battle between the raiders and his crew.

"He's saving us. All of us."

"Crew don't seem to think so." Judge shifted his hand from rubbing his beard to rubbing his paunchy stomach. "They might force him off the *Lucky*."

"You can prevent that." She realized her hand was holding the knife out in front of her, like a threat. She lowered it.

"I don't think I can. These men are superstitious. And your friend is… well, he's going wild."

Vellory looked at where Corky was. She caught glimpses of him, here and there, between the shifting tide of crew and raiders between her and her twin.

"He's going to kill the raiders." Judge said it matter-of-factly. As if it was an undeniable fact. She agreed with him.

"And then, if he can manage his powers, he'll settle down." Judge arched a brow. It seemed he wanted her to speak.

"He'll be fine. He's saving our lives."

Gillings, who'd been standing silently next to his boss, cut in. "Power does strange things to grown men, and he's but a boy. I'd wager we're all about to die."

Vellory snapped at the reeking man. "Then why are you still standing here?"

"What should I do? Flee?" Gillings asked, laughing. "Where would I go? And what sort of first mate would I be if I left Judge and the *Lucky?* If I survived, I'd lose all credibility. No," he said, shaking his head, "a man's gotta make a stand."

"You're standing here, all right," Vellory said. "But I can't say you're doing anything to improve the situation."

Gillings glared at her.

"Enough," Judge said. "We'll wait it out. See what happens. Mother Avani will take care of us. And, if not," Judge stopped, issuing a hopeful look up at the sky, "then it's just our time to go."

Vellory didn't expect Judge to be a pious man, but there it was. She shrugged and searched the swathes of men looking for Corky.

The ferry shifted. Either from men running across the boat, or from Corky's powers, she didn't know. Half the crew onboard tumbled to their hands and knees, and Vellory herself found her face below her feet, rebounding off the wooden planking. A gash in her forehead poured blood and tears in her eyes blinded her for a moment. Her head ringing, she just lay there for a moment. Pain coursed its way through her body and she screamed, but she wasn't sure if it was because of pain, a feeling of helplessness, or concern for her friend. Vellory just needed to get something *out.* She wiped her eyes clear of tears, then had to wipe them clear again from blood.

Blinking, she sat up, leaning against a crate that had slid

across the ferry to rest nearby. With the crate, a fresh trail of blood had streaked across the decking, dragged along by the box. She saw flesh sticking to a corner and averted her gaze. Stars swam in her vision, and clarity kept disappearing. Something wasn't right. Something inside her head felt off. Fuzzy. Distant. She groaned.

The loud noises of the ship, the men, the swords, screams of pain, and shouts for help, the constant ringing in her ears. The ringing. Endless ringing. She groaned and cradled her head between her hands. The sounds of whatever the fuck Corky was doing mixed with splashing water and frothing rapids. The ferry had drifted into faster waters, and now was buckling up and down, back and forth.

Her head pulsed, and she groaned. Her eyes heavy, she closed them. She wanted to drift off to sleep. She blinked again, saw chaos. Vellory recognized the body that lay a few feet in front of her. His spiky, oiled hair gave him away. *Pasco,* she thought. *Pasco.* She couldn't remember how she knew the man, but she knew the name. Knew he wasn't standing back up. She could see inside his chest. Vellory almost giggled at that, wondered why. Her vision went black again. The ringing in her ears intensified. She couldn't hear other noises now. She blinked, blinked again. Blinked a third time. Exhaustion washed over her.

"Mum," she said. "Dad." She coughed. "Good night."

She slept.

Corkel snarled. He burned, he killed, he destroyed. He gnashed his teeth and destroyed everyone. Anger blossomed inside. A fire he couldn't control. One, upon reflection, he noticed his father possessed when he'd slipped too deep into the drink.

He slashed his hand through the air. A bladed arc tore

through the air, slicing men down like a sickle cuts wheat. He grinned. The power. He was indestructible. A silly man thought to take him down with an arrow again. He built a bubble around himself, and the arrow bounced off it, snapping in half.

Corkel turned his attention to the man who'd released the arrow. He clapped and the man exploded into bits of flesh and bone. The dust of a man.

Nobody could get near him. He snorted at their pathetic attempts, and he slayed them all.

A man ran towards him, both hands held up. Corkel saw no weapon, but dispatched the man. *Trickery*. Nobody would trick Corkel. He'd spent his entire life as a scrawny, weak boy who'd relied on his best friend, a woman, to protect him. Other men saw him as pathetic. As emasculated. He'd show them.

He turned to face the crowd. His face warped into a snarl, and he ground his teeth, displaying his ferocity to them. Corkel saw some of them drop to their knees, issuing prayers. *Prayers. PRAY TO ME!* He wished he'd voiced his thoughts aloud, but there was little point. They'd all be dead soon. All of them. Dead.

He burned and he impaled. He drowned and he electrocuted. Corkel's eyes narrowed, and he looked at his opponents in disgust. He ruined them. His boots slipped in blood and gore and dead bodies, and twice he almost tripped.

A smelly man, a man who immediately disgusted Corkel, dropped to all fours in front of him. Tears streamed down his face.

"You don't disrespect me!" Corkel said, and he split the man clean in half from his groin up through his head. Brain and guts and flesh popped up in the air, like a ripe fruit splitting with a bit too much force.

It felt good. Good to consume his power. Good to ruin

those around him. It was good to show everyone he wasn't just a *boy.*

A wispy thought of a girl passed through his mind, but he ignored it. Right now, there were only men. The men who had wanted to kill him. And now he was killing them. And they begged for their lives.

But he wouldn't let them have what they wanted. He denied their pleas. Their prostrations. Their life.

A squat man with a patchy beard was next. He hadn't pleaded or prostrated. He'd started running towards the edge of the ferry. As he leaped, Corkel brought his hand down, and a force of air smacked the man into the water so strongly, it was as if he'd fallen from the sky. His body exploded on the water's top, and the bits that remained floated along with the current.

And then it was done. Corkel didn't see anyone else. There was nobody left to kill.

All of them.

He waded through the blood, bone, and gore, like he was catching frogs at the edge of a pond. He'd done that, once. Catch frogs. Catching frogs was more difficult than what he'd done here.

His sanity recuperated. Corkel blinked. Recognition bled into his awareness. Wholesale slaughter. Everyone… dead.

"Vel?" he whispered. "Vel?" He didn't want to find her. Didn't want to see what he'd done to her. Corkel started sweating. His hands trembled, so he clenched them into fists, which didn't help because his arms started trembling instead. He unclasped his hands and, shaking, looked around the *Lucky Lucard.* A swirl of red. No sounds. There wouldn't be sounds because nobody was alive to make it. The tinkling of water, a splash of wave, something rolling up and down the deck. Nothing more.

"Vel?" he asked again. "Vel?" He needed to find her. Had to make sure she was okay. But. *What if she saw everything?*

What if… he couldn't finish the thought. A monster. That's what he was. Corkel shook his head. He'd killed everyone. Not just the raiders, but everyone. He had a sudden need to vomit, and he plunged his head under the railing and over the side of the ferry, spewing his stomach's contents into the water and against the ferry's siding.

He waited a few moments for the ferry to drift away from his excretions. Then he dipped his hand into the water, cupping it into his mouth. He drank. And drank. He filled his stomach with water, and yet, he was still thirsty. And tired. He was so exhausted. Drained.

Corkel stood, leaning against the rail. The *Lucky* kept drifting down the river. He wondered what anyone would do should they witness this unholy sight. He glanced back at the bodies, gagged, and looked away. There was no doubt about it. *He'd* done this. Him. Corkel Rebbins. A small, scrawny little boy. He looked at his arms. Hairy and thick. They weren't boy arms anymore.

Curious and afraid, he peered into the river. A shimmering man stared back at him. A man who'd seen a hard life. Flecks of gray dotted his beard. Weathered lines had carved runnels across his forehead. Corkel guessed he looked like a forty-year-old man who'd spent his life farming. He looked away and collapsed on the deck. His legs, much longer now than this morning, stretched out in front of him like a pair of giant stilts.

"What happened?" he asked himself. "What happened?" He'd lost decades of his life. He knew why: his power. It had to come from somewhere. It aged him? Vellory had been right. And now he'd sapped so much of his life. He wondered if Magicai suffered the same fate. He wondered if they'd been able to teach him, if he'd been able to control it. Corkel didn't have the answers. Didn't much care. Not much they could do for him now.

He made a vow to never use his power again.

He had to find Vellory. Corkel rose from the deck and started searching the *Lucky*. The ferry wasn't huge. It wasn't a strenuous task. It wouldn't take too long to search everywhere. But it was taxing to see the damage he'd caused, the bodies—or lack of whole bodies, really. Gore splattered every foot of the deck, coating the barrels and the crates. The slick surface was difficult to navigate. Bile rose in his throat again, but he choked it back down.

"Vel?" he said, peeking around the three barrels of fruit they'd hidden behind. He spied Bonebreaker, and a sword lodged in it. He pried the sword loose, tossing it overboard, and held Bonebreaker in both hands. Corkel sent a prayer to Mother Avani that this wouldn't be the only thing left of her. *Please. Please be okay.*

He navigated through the deeper mass of body parts and other unidentifiable sludge. *Body... remnants.* He tried not to think about it, just searched. And then he found her. It'd taken him longer to find her, because her body leaned against a crate, and a second crate had obscured her. Corkel closed the distance, kneeling in the mess beside her. Vellory's face was caked with dried blood. He leaned close, heard the faintest whisper of a breath escaping her half-open mouth.

She was dying.

"No, no, no, no," he said. Corkel reached down, grabbed her tiny hand with his large ones. He held her hand, rubbing the back of hers with his thumb. "Please, Vel, wake up. Wake up, Vel. Don't die on me. I'm sorry. I'm so sorry. It's all my fault." Tears flowed from his eyes.

Her shallowing breathing was so weak. She had a gash in her forehead and, when he looked closely, he swore he saw her skull protruding from the flesh. He grimaced, then reached up, pulling the wound apart. For a second, he caught sight of a crack on the bone, then a fresh wave of blood poured forth.

Corkel needed to help her. He didn't know how. Didn't

know what to do. He remembered back when he'd first discovered his power. He'd somehow unlocked something inside of him. Corkel didn't know how that happened. It just had. When he'd somehow stumbled upon it. He'd just felt something snap inside of him. Or connect. But somehow, it'd happened. He reached within, searching, hoping, wondering if there was some way he could shift that power to fix, rather than destroy.

He prayed, begged, and hoped. But nothing happened. Vellory's breathing grew weaker. Her pulse struggled. He tried harder. He held her against him, and he tried.

Something changed after a moment. A link formed. He felt her pain, could identify every wound. A fractured skull. The open wounds and several bruises. He even sensed brain damage. This was a new sensation, something he didn't know he was capable of. Something in him changed, as though he'd been granted access to something new. He no longer doubted he could fix things.

But he'd promised himself. No more powers.

"Vel," he said. He swallowed. Corkel had two choices. He knew that. Three, if he wanted to end up on the wrong end of a noose.

The first, he abides by his original promise. No more powers. Vellory dies.

The second, he fixes her, except her brain damage. He could tell she was going to suffer long-term damage. It'd ruin her memory. But he'd care for her.

The third, he could completely heal her. But he knew what'd happen if he did. She'd rat him out. He'd die.

At that moment, he realized how selfish he was. He couldn't do option three, even if it was the best one for her. Corkel didn't want to die. He was a man now. Nobody would coddle him like he was a weak, scrawny child.

He closed his eyes, his decision made. Corkel used his powers to take away her brain's swelling. He repaired the cracked skull, and he closed all her open wounds, and took away every bruise her body possessed. He left the brain damage.

Cradling her limp, but healed body in his arms, he carried her off the *Lucky Lucard*. Carried her into the wilds.

Together, he knew, they'd live a happy life. Perhaps not a long one. He'd seen his reflection in the waters as he'd fled the ferry. He'd become an old man. Vellory would be his brain-damaged child, Corkel, her grandfather. He'd take care of her.

And he wouldn't die a criminal.

ABOUT THE AUTHOR

You've stumbled upon somebody who takes nothing seriously, not even author bios. It'd be a good guess to say John Palladino was born in 1988, lives in Avoca, New York, has a bachelor's degree in business management, and enjoys hibernating at home while writing. He might also lie and say he enjoys pets, long walks on the beach, and his hobbies include happiness and scuba diving. You'd see right through those lies, however, and notice he prefers the simpler things in life—reading, video games, and making ill-timed jokes. John also dislikes taking care of anything that excretes substances.

www.ingramcontent.com/pod-product-compliance
Lightning Source LLC
Chambersburg PA
CBHW031120130726
47988CB00006B/2155